P9-DIE-885

THE SADDLE CLUB

SADDLE SORE

BONNIE BRYANT

A SKYLARK BOOK

NEW YORK • TORONTO • LONDON • SYDNEY • AUCKLAND

RL 5, 009–012

SADDLE SORE

A Bantam Skylark Book / June 1997

ISBN 0-553-48421-4

Published simultaneously in the United States and Canada.

PRINTED IN THE UNITED STATES OF AMERICA

OPM   0 9 8 7 6 5 4 3 2 1

I would like to express my special thanks to Kimberly Brubaker Bradley for her help in the writing of this book.

1

"Look! You can see the mountains!" Emily Williams leaned forward, pressing her face against the pane of one of the plane's small windows. "Some of them still have snow."

"The Bar None isn't that high up," Emily's friend Lisa Atwood assured her. "We won't be riding through snow."

Emily sat back. "That's good, I guess, since I only brought summer clothes. But riding through snow is fun!"

"Riding through sagebrush is fun, too," a third friend, Carole Hanson, said.

"Well, I don't know about riding *through* sagebrush," joked the final girl in the cabin, Stevie Lake. "Riding *near* sagebrush, maybe. Riding around it. Riding past it and admiring the sagebrush—that's fun. But riding *through* sagebrush hurts! It's prickly."

"I'll write that down so I don't forget it," Emily said dryly. The others laughed. It was hard for them all not to laugh, when they knew they were on their way to have a great time riding at the Bar None ranch.

Lisa, Carole, and Stevie had been best friends for a very long time. They were all completely horse-crazy, and, in fact, they had met at Pine Hollow, a riding stable in Willow Creek, Virginia, where they all rode. When they discovered how much they had in common, they formed The Saddle Club. Its only two rules were that members had to help each other out, and they had to be totally, irredeemably, horse-crazy.

They hadn't known Emily Williams for that long, but already she was one of their close friends. Because she had cerebral palsy, Emily rode at the Free Rein Therapeutic Riding Center, a place for disabled riders. She was a very good rider. She even had her own horse, a loving palomino named P.C. Sometimes Emily came to

Pine Hollow to ride, but she kept P.C. at Free Rein.

"You won't believe it, Emily," Carole said, her dark eyes shining with excitement. "The land is so open—you won't see a fence for miles."

"Oh, please," Stevie retorted. "The only way she won't see a fence is if she shuts her eyes. Em, they keep the horses in paddocks close to the barns, just the way you'd expect. They've got a little pasture for grazing, too, next to the ranch house, and they've got wire fences strung around the whole property. Otherwise the cows could just mosey into town."

"And Mrs. Devine's garden is fenced, too," Lisa remembered.

"Otherwise the cows would eat lettuce for lunch," Stevie said.

"Please!" Carole said, aiming a firm smile at Stevie. "You know exactly what I mean, and Emily does, too. Of course there are fences. There just don't *seem* to be any. We can ride for miles, and if we ride in the right direction, there's nothing to stop us at all."

"Except a nasty bunch of sagebrush," Stevie murmured, and they all laughed. Of the three Saddle Club members, Stevie was the most playful, and she loved all sorts of jokes. Stevie's plans often landed them all in hot water, but her cleverness just as often bailed them out.

"So if my horse bucks me off, it'll be able to run for miles," Emily said. "You're right, Carole, that is something to look forward to." She said it with a laugh, and the others laughed in response.

Emily's personality was a lot like Stevie's. Both liked to have fun, but both could be incredibly stubborn. Emily's stubbornness often worked to her advantage—she kept trying a thing until she did it.

"A Bar None horse would never buck a rider off," Carole protested. "Wait until you meet them, Emily. They're the sweetest horses in the world."

If the others were horse-crazy, Carole was horse-berserk. Someday, her friends were sure, Carole would do great things in the horse world, but for now she contented herself with learning every single thing possible about them and spending all of her free time around them.

"Better than P.C.?" Emily asked. "Better than Starlight?" Starlight was Carole's own horse.

"Well, no, of course not," Carole amended.

"But aside from P.C. and Starlight, they're the sweetest horses—"

"What about Belle?" Stevie demanded, at the same time as Lisa said, "What about Prancer?" Belle was Stevie's horse; Prancer was the lesson horse Lisa usually rode.

"Sorry," Carole said. "Okay, aside from P.C., Starlight, Belle, and Prancer—"

"What about Topside?" Stevie asked. Lisa added, "What about Delilah?" Both were favorite Pine Hollow horses.

Emily laughed. So did Carole. "I guess you'd better just say they have very sweet horses at the Bar None," Emily said.

"That's right," Carole said. "I'd better not draw comparisons. I couldn't, anyway. Horses are all so different, like people."

"Emily, you'll love it," Lisa said softly. She was the quietest and most academic member of The Saddle Club. "I remember the first time I came to the Bar None. I really hadn't been riding for very long then, and I had never imagined a place like it."

"I have," Emily replied. "I've been dreaming and daydreaming about this trip ever since I learned we were going." Then she laughed again and tossed back her short dark hair. "I have to admit, I think Pine Hollow is pretty close to perfect, because of all the trails! It's hard to believe that this place will be even better. And I *can't* believe I'm here on this plane with you guys. It's amazing."

"Colonel Devine wanted to thank you," Carole said. "He told us you helped him a lot."

The Devines owned the Bar None and ran it as a dude ranch. Colonel Frank Devine was one of Carole's father's friends. His daughter, Kate, had first been Carole's good friend; now she was an auxiliary member of The Saddle Club. Colonel Devine had been a pilot in the Marines and still did some flying for corporations out West. Whenever he came to the East Coast, he tried to arrange a get-together for Kate and The Saddle Club.

The Bar None had become a popular vacation spot for families. Last spring Colonel Devine had called Carole to explain that he wanted to expand their facilities. Many of his former Marine Corps buddies were veterans of the Vietnam War, and a number of them were disabled. He wanted them to be able to enjoy the ranch, too, so he was taking steps to make the Bar None accessible to everyone. Kate had told him about The Saddle Club's work at Free Rein and the friend they had made there. Could he talk to Emily?

Carole had given him Emily's phone number, and later Emily had told her they'd had a long conversation. Frank Devine had already been in touch with several national organizations for the disabled, she said, including the North American Riding for the Handicapped Association, or NARHA, which oversaw therapeutic riding organizations. But he had some specific questions to ask a rider, and she'd been able to answer most of them. A few months later, he'd invited them all West for a week, including Emily. Colonel Devine was flying the small plane they were in now, taking them to Kate and the ranch.

"He wanted to thank me, but he said he wants to get some work out of me, too," Emily said. "He wants my opinion on his improvements." She grinned. "This is going to be really fun."

"Passengers, prepare for landing." Colonel Devine's voice was stern over the intercom.

Emily giggled. "Does he always sound like that?"

Stevie nodded. "When he's flying, he becomes this whole other person, Colonel Invincible, Captain of the Skies. Don't worry. At the Bar None he's a regular dad."

"He seemed regular before the plane took off," Emily said.

They gathered the books and snacks they'd spread about the small cabin and zipped their backpacks closed. Emily fit the cuffs of her crutches over her forearms. To walk she needed both crutches and leg braces, but to ride horses she didn't need either. She had a wheelchair, but she avoided using it whenever she could.

When the little plane landed, Colonel Devine had no sooner dropped the ramp down when a tall girl came flying up it. "Stevie!" she shrieked. "Carole! Lisa! *Emily!*" She gave them each a hug, nearly knocking Emily down.

"Kate!" they all shrieked back.

"Come on, let's go!" Kate said, grabbing backpacks and hurrying them out the door. "My mom's in the truck, she's dying to meet you, Emily. We brought snacks in case you're hungry, and John says hi to all of you. If we get back quickly we can ride before dinner, and, oh, Carole, wait

8

until you see the new foals!" Kate clattered down the ramp.

Emily burst out laughing. "You're right, Carole," she said. "You said I'd feel like I knew her right away, and I do. Who's John?"

"He works at the Bar None—he and his dad. He's our age." Lisa's eyes were shining. She liked John Brightstar quite a lot. They all did, but Lisa liked him the most.

Emily made her way slowly and carefully down the ramp. None of The Saddle Club offered to help her, and neither, they noted with satisfaction, did Kate. Emily was very firm about doing things for herself.

Before long they were all on their way to the ranch. The drive was barely long enough to exchange all the news with Kate. Before long they were talking about horses.

"This is P.C." Emily pulled a photograph out of her backpack. "I knew you'd want to see what he looked like, so I brought this. It's his summer coat, fortunately. In winter he looks like a yellow bear."

"He's adorable!" Kate said. "Look how nice his expression is."

"He's perfect for me," Emily said. "He tries to do everything I ask."

"Emily even taught him to lie down on command," Stevie bragged. "She uses it for mounting and dismounting whenever there isn't a ramp around." Emily couldn't lift her foot high enough to mount a horse from the ground.

Emily grinned. "We all taught him that, Stevie, and it was your idea in the first place. But he does do it whenever I need him to."

"Well, we haven't got any lying-down horses at the ranch yet," Kate said. "Moonglow does most other things, though. I can't make up my mind what sort of horse I want her to be, so right now I've got her jumping logs, schooling trot extensions and collections, and working on spins."

The others laughed. Trot extensions and collections were advanced English-style riding; spins were advanced Western. "What sort of saddle are you riding her in?" Carole asked.

Kate shrugged. "Usually Western, but sometimes English."

"I didn't think you were jumping much out here," Lisa added.

Kate shrugged again, this time with a wide

grin. "You see a log, you might as well jump it," she said. "Moonglow seems to think so, too." Kate had gotten Moonglow from a government sale of wild horses. Moonglow's training had been an extensive project that Kate thoroughly enjoyed. Before her parents bought the ranch, Kate had been a top competitive junior rider, but her drive to win had taken all the fun out of riding for her. She'd given riding up entirely, until she met The Saddle Club; now she rode strictly for fun.

"We'll have to see some logs, then," Carole said. She loved jumping. "Kate, we came to an agreement on the plane. Emily's never ridden in a place like this, and we haven't been here for a long time. So we're going to ride all week long."

Kate looked surprised. "Do you ever do anything else?"

"Well, sometimes—"

"This week we're not doing *anything* but riding," Stevie cut in.

"Ride, ride, ride," Lisa said.

"Great!" said Kate.

Emily grinned. Her friends could see how thrilled she was.

"So, Emily," Mrs. Devine said, over the back of the front seat, "did Frank tell you all about our improvements?"

"No, he just told me to fasten my seat belt. What's new?"

They talked for a while about the ramps added to all the buildings, for wheelchair entrance, the enlarged doorways in some of the bunkhouses, and other modifications the Devines had made. Kate told them excitedly about the retraining program she and John Brightstar had undertaken with some of the ranch saddle horses.

"We tried to do everything the people from NARHA told us about," she said. "Getting them used to the mounting ramp and being mounted from either side, getting them to move off voice and stick commands, as well as leg commands— everything. Plus, of course, making sure they're super calm. We've got two or three horses we think are completely ready, and several more are coming along.

"Emily, I'm going to give you Spot for the week. He used to be my horse, until I got Moon-glow, and he's got wonderful gaits and a great disposition. You're going to love him. He's an Appaloosa."

Emily grinned. "Thanks, Kate. I'm sure I'll love him."

"One of our mares is doing amazingly well," Kate continued. "Her name is Buttercup. I've been working with her a lot, because I want her to be ready for Monica. Monica always rides Buttercup when she comes here." Kate's voice dropped to a sad tone. "I haven't told you about Monica."

Mrs. Devine looked over the back of her seat again. "Such a tragedy. And they'll be here tomorrow."

"Who?" asked Lisa.

"Monica and her parents," Kate replied. "See, they started coming here the first year we opened the ranch, and they loved it so much they came back every year. Monica's our age. She's funny and athletic, and a great rider. We got to be pretty good friends.

"She had an accident on a motorbike last fall. It crushed her lower leg, and they had to amputate it. Her parents had already made their reservations to come here. They told Mom they wanted to cancel, but Monica wouldn't let them. She wants everything in her life to be the same as it used to be."

Kate's eyes filled with tears. "I wanted to have disabled people come to the ranch, but I didn't want that to mean Monica! I mean—of course I'm glad she's coming, I'm just so sorry this happened to her."

Carole patted Kate's leg sympathetically. Lisa gave her shoulder a squeeze. "It sounds terrible," Stevie said. "We'll just have to do all we can to make sure she has a really good time."

"If she was a good rider before, she should still be a good rider," Emily said. "Does she have an artificial leg?"

Kate blinked. "I don't know."

Mr. Devine shook his head. "I don't think so. I think it's still too soon."

"That's too bad," Emily said. "What about her knee? Did they save her knee?"

Lisa burst out laughing. "Emily, what a question! You sound so practical—in a ghoulish sort of way."

Emily shook her head. "Think about it. If she still has a knee, her seat in the saddle will feel pretty normal. Otherwise it will be harder for her to balance, without an artificial leg."

"She still has her knee," Kate confirmed. "I didn't talk to her—she was still at the rehab hospital when her mother called here—but her mom said it was just her lower leg."

Emily nodded. "Good. She can use a crop for leg commands, the way I do, but she should be able to adjust quickly. She'll be able to ride every day, just like us."

"The more the merrier," Stevie said, and the others agreed.

Colonel Devine pulled the truck to a stop in front of the ranch house. "Home, sweet home," he said.

The girls piled out. "C'mon!" Kate said. "Let's go see the horses!"

"What about your luggage, hmm?" her father asked. "Or maybe Emily wants a glass of water. Have you thought about that?"

"Oh, the luggage!" Lisa stopped in her tracks. "I suppose—"

Kate pulled her forward. "He's joking! Don't worry about it! Only—"

"I'm not thirsty," Emily said, walking forward without a backward glance. "Which barn has my horse in it?"

As they approached the horse barn, a tall, dark-haired boy in a cowboy hat and blue jeans came out to greet them. "Hi, everybody," he said softly. "Hi, Lisa."

"Hi," Lisa returned. "Emily, this is John Brightstar. John, this is Emily Williams."

John tipped his hat. "Pleased to meet you, Emily," he said. "I've been working Spot for you. Want to try him out?"

"Right now?"

"Why not?"

Emily beamed. "Wonderful!"

They entered the big, high-ceilinged barn. Inside, the air was rich with the fragrance of hay. Only one horse stood in the stalls inside.

"Where's Stewball?" Stevie demanded. Stewball was the horse she always rode at the Bar None. "You've made poor Spot stay inside by himself! Where are all the others?"

"Outside, where they belong," John replied. "And poor Spot has only been inside for ten minutes, since I saw Kate's dad's truck turn off the road. I haven't even gotten him groomed yet."

"That's good," Emily said. "I'd rather groom him myself, so I can get to know him." She walked to the door of the stall and held her hands out so that Spot could sniff them.

"Here's what John and I thought," Kate said to The Saddle Club. "Emily's never ridden Western, which is a little different, and she's used to her own horse, not Spot. So—sorry, Stevie, if this disappoints you—we thought just Emily should ride right now, in the paddock, to get used to things. We can all show her how to do it. Then tomorrow we'll head for the trails, where we belong."

"That sounds perfect," Carole said.

"I agree," Stevie said. "Just let me duck outside and tell Stewball about it. I wouldn't want him to think I was ignoring him." She went out the back door.

Emily attached a lead rope to Spot's halter and led him into the aisle. She tied him there so that she could groom him. "Is Stevie always that way about Stewball? She talked about him the whole trip, but she never actually told me what he was like."

"Put it this way," Lisa said. "Stevie and Stewball are *exactly* alike."

"Oh." Emily chuckled softly.

Kate came out of the tack room with a bucket of grooming supplies in her hand, a Western bridle slung over her shoulder, and a heavy Western saddle over her arm. Carole and Lisa quickly relieved her of saddle and bridle. Kate handed the grooming bucket to Emily.

Emily took a rubber curry out of it, then set the bucket down on the ground. She had to maneuver carefully around it so that she wouldn't hit it with the tip of a crutch. "Here's an improvement for you," she said. "See, Kate? I'm going to have an awful time getting stuff in and out of that bucket. When I bend over I sometimes lose my balance. At Free Rein, we've got a little shelf to keep stuff like this at waist level. Your dad could build one in here."

"I'll tell him," Kate said. "That's a good idea."

"When Emily comes to Pine Hollow, we use a hay bale," Carole said. She dragged one within Emily's reach and put the bucket on it.

"Thanks," Emily told her.

Carole grabbed a brush and went around to Spot's other side. She started untangling his mane, humming as she did so. It felt so great to be back at the Bar None, surrounded by horses, mountains, and friends. But not in that order. Maybe friends, horses, mountains? Horses, friends, mountains? It was hard to decide. The mountains were definitely the least important, so they should go last. Friends were most important, so probably they should come first. But then horses were important, too, and the Devines had so many horses, they really outnumbered the friends. Maybe horses should be first, because there were so many of them. Carole laughed.

"What's so funny?" Emily came around Spot's rump and started to curry his withers.

"I'm trying to decide what friends are worth in terms of horses," Carole said. "If I have four friends here, how many is that in horses? The Devines have nearly a hundred horses—but maybe foals don't count as much—"

"How good are the horses?" Emily asked.

"Very good."

"How good are the friends?" Kate chimed in.

"The best."

"Then each friend is worth thirty-two point two five horses," Emily said. "So unless you've got more than, uh—"

"One hundred twenty-nine," Lisa said. She was good at math.

"One hundred twenty-nine horses here—we're still worth more."

"Sorry, Carole," Kate said. "Last count was seventy-eight horses, including foals."

Stevie came back in time to hear most of this. "Stewball counts quadruple," she said. She picked up a comb and started on Spot's tail. Lisa was picking out Spot's feet. Emily traded the curry for a large body brush and began brushing the dirt from Spot's flanks.

"Hey," Kate protested to The Saddle Club, "the only reason I didn't grab a brush is that you guys told me Emily didn't like to be helped. Now there's nothing left for me to do!"

"You could brush his face with the soft brush," Emily suggested. She went on to explain. "They're right, I do like to do things for myself. It drives me crazy when people rush in to help me because they think I can't do something, or because I'm doing it more slowly than they would. But two things make this different: First, you guys are my friends, and even when you're helping me I know you know I'm capable of things. Second, Kate, this is The Saddle Club. Have you ever

21

seen them stand near a horse and not try to groom it? You should have been there the first time they met P.C. They practically had to sit on their hands not to touch him."

Kate laughed. Carole said, "She's got us figured out."

Lisa had just started to wonder where John had gone when he came in through the back door. "I watered the paddock down," he said. "It's dusty out there. Is Emily ready?"

Kate finished explaining the intricacies of a Western girth to Emily. It was the only thing truly different about saddling up a horse Western. "We're ready," Kate said.

Emily led Spot outside. Though she walked slowly, Spot kept his head level with his shoulder, just as he should. "Good boy," Emily murmured.

"He's always been this good," Kate said proudly.

John showed off the mounting ramp he had built. It was a wooden platform about two feet high. On one side it had steps, like a regular mounting block, but on the other side it had a long, shallow ramp.

Emily started up the ramp. Steps were almost always too high for her to climb. "This is great," she said. "Only, John, you might want to add a handrail to both sides, not just one. I don't need it, but some of your other guests might."

John nodded. "I didn't think of that. I have been teaching the horses to get used to being mounted from either side." Horses were almost always mounted from the left side only, but some riders with disabilities found it easier to mount from the right.

Kate helped hold Spot still in front of the block while Emily unfastened her leg braces and set her crutches down. She held on to Spot's mane and the back of his saddle for support.

"The stirrups look different," she said.

"That's because they're made of wood," Kate explained. "They won't feel much different, except that in Western riding you usually ride with your stirrups a little lower."

"Did you remember to bring your crop?" Lisa asked. Emily showed it to her. "Good," Lisa said. Crops weren't generally used in Western riding, but Emily always rode with one because she had trouble moving her legs to give the horse the correct signals. She gave them with the crop instead. She called her crop her third leg.

"We've been using a crop on Spot for a couple of weeks now," Kate informed her. "He should be thoroughly used to it."

"All aboard," Stevie said.

Emily grinned. She carefully climbed into the saddle and settled her feet in the stirrups. She picked up the reins, and Kate moved away from Spot's head. Spot stood still, waiting for Emily's signal.

Emily looked around with mock dismay. "Help! I never thought about this. How do I ask a Western horse to walk?"

"How do you think?" Stevie asked.

"How should I know? I might have to pull his tail or something!"

Kate laughed. "It's the same as English riding," she said. "The horses are trained to the same cues. Just pretend you're riding P.C."

Emily nodded. "That's a relief. I'm not sure I could reach his tail." She signaled Spot to walk and pointed him toward the rail. "This saddle's comfortable. It's much more like a chair than my saddle at home. How do I look?"

The Saddle Club, Kate, and John surveyed her critically. "You tell her," Kate said to John.

"Oh, no," Emily said. "Sounds like I'm doing something wrong."

"You look relaxed and comfortable," John said, "but you're holding your reins in both hands."

"What should I be doing? Holding them with my feet? Draping them around my neck? Hands seem like the obvious choice here."

"Hand," Stevie said. "Hand, not hands. Put both reins in one hand, and keep them loose."

"Like a cowboy," Emily said.

"You *are* a cowboy now," Kate said.

Emily grinned. "I never thought of that." She walked Spot several times around the arena. "Feels good. What else?"

"Move your rein hand so that your left rein drapes across his neck," John directed. Emily did. Spot instantly swung to the right, away from the rein.

"Wow!" Emily cried. "He turned!"

"Sure." Kate looked proud. "That's called neck reining, and most Western horses do it. Spot does it very well."

"Cool beans," Emily said. She neck-reined

Spot in a serpentine pattern around the arena. Then, following John's instructions, she jogged and then loped around the arena. A jog was a Western trot, and a lope was a Western canter. She did circles and changed directions at all three gaits. She looked easy and confident, and Spot obeyed her perfectly.

A loud bell rang across the ranch. Emily eased Spot to a halt. "That wouldn't be—by any chance—a dinner bell?" Kate nodded. Emily beamed. "I love the West!" she shouted. "Get along, little dogies! Let's eat!"

With all of them working together, it didn't take long to untack Spot and turn him out with the other riding horses. John and his father left for home. Soon the rest of them were all sitting at one of the long tables in the ranch house dining room. Kate's parents joined them for a hearty meal. No one else was in the room. Mrs. Devine explained to them that the only other visitors right now were two honeymoon couples, both of whom had requested picnic dinners to take on sunset rides.

"That's all they've done since they got here," Kate said. "We hardly see them at all."

"They aren't much work, but they aren't much

company, either," Mrs. Devine agreed. "I'm glad all you girls could come. And tomorrow, of course, we'll be joined by the Hopkins family."

"That's Monica and her parents," Kate explained.

After they helped with the dinner dishes and said good night to the Colonel and Mrs. Devine, Kate took them to the four-person bunkhouse they always stayed in. "This week it sleeps five," Kate said as she opened the door. "I added a cot."

"Kate always stays with us," Lisa explained to Emily.

"Good," Emily said.

Aside from the fold-out cot, Lisa noticed a few other small changes to the familiar bunkhouse. A new ramp had been added to the side of the porch, to supplement the steps, a wedge of wood had smoothed the step up to the door, and the door was wider. In the small bathroom, rails had been added near the toilet and bathtub. All of these would make it more usable for Emily and the other disabled visitors who would come.

Colonel Devine had brought their bags in and dumped them on the beds. Emily's wheelchair was folded and stored beneath a bunk. "Let's leave it there," Emily said, pushing it farther under. "I'm not using the stupid thing once this week."

"You won't have to," Stevie said. "You'll be riding everywhere we go."

Lisa yawned. "I hate to say I'm tired, but . . ." She yawned again.

Stevie yawned in response, and then Emily did. Carole shook her head. She opened her mouth to say something but yawned instead. "It's contagious," Kate said. She yawned, too. "I don't know why I should be tired." She yawned once more. "But I guess I am."

"The sooner we go to sleep, the sooner we can get up and ride," Lisa suggested. The others thought this was a perfect example of Lisa's best logic. Before long they were all in their pajamas, crawling into the bunks.

"I keep thinking about Monica," Kate confessed, as she passed around a box of cookies her mother had given her. "I'm really excited about seeing her, but I'm sort of dreading it, too. I want her to have a fun time here. I don't want it to be different from the way it used to be. What I really want is for her accident not to have happened. She was so lively—I think one day we rode for eight hours straight. And once we hung a rope from the barn rafter and took turns swinging into this big pile of hay. And we used to laugh together all the time."

Lisa tried to comfort Kate. "She'll still laugh. She'll be the same person—she lost a leg, that's all. She didn't lose her personality."

"I don't know about that," Stevie said. "I mean, of course she'll still have a personality; I'm just not sure she'll be exactly the same. Like the people you read about in books, the dark heroes whose lives have been overshadowed by tragedy. It colors the soul."

"Like Heathcliff," Kate said. "Maybe."

"No, Heathcliff's a cat," Stevie said. "I'm talking real tragedy."

"Heathcliff's not a cat," Kate said indignantly. "Honestly, Stevie!"

"He's a guy in an old movie," Carole explained. "I saw it one night with my dad. He was played by somebody famous, I think, but it was in black and white."

"He's a person!" Kate said. "I mean, a character. In a book I read, *Wuthering Heights*. His life was overcome with sorrow."

"So he wasn't as nice, then?" Lisa asked.

"He wasn't all that nice to begin with," Kate admitted. "What do you think, Emily?"

Emily propped herself up on her elbow. "I don't have any idea how Monica will be," she said. "I've never met her. But if the accident just happened recently, I'm sure she'll still be upset about it. I would be. I think anyone would be."

"I am, and it didn't even happen to me," Kate said. "I guess the only thing we can do about it is make sure she has as nice a time as possible."

"We're all going to have a great time," Carole said. "I love it out here, Kate."

Emily flopped back against her pillow. "A whole week with nothing to do but ride!" she said. "I never imagined anything so wonderful!"

3

THE NEXT MORNING, after breakfast, the girls followed Kate out to the paddock beside the barn, where a dozen or so of the ranch riding horses had spent the night. John Brightstar was already there, haltering a gorgeous chestnut gelding.

Lisa went up to greet him. "Tex looks marvelous!" she said. "He's really added some muscle since we saw him last."

John smiled proudly. "He needs it now. You should see what he can do." Tex was John's horse, and John had been training him to do

31

reining, the most precise and elegant form of Western riding. Reining was similar to dressage in English riding.

"Come with us," Lisa said. "We're going to warm up in the side paddock for a few minutes, and then we're taking Emily on her first Western trail ride."

John smiled wryly. "Why do you think I'm out here?" he asked. "Kate already invited me. I even got up early, to get my work done first."

"Great," Lisa said. Something about the way John smiled always made her stomach feel pleasantly uneasy. She often wished John lived a little closer—like, in Willow Creek, or at least in the state of Virginia. Sometimes they wrote to each other, but it was hard to keep a long-distance friendship going.

"I'll put Tex in the barn and help you guys get your horses out," he offered. He walked away, and Lisa turned back to her friends.

Emily and Carole were standing just outside the gate, waiting with lead ropes in their hands. Kate had gone into the paddock to separate out their horses. Stevie was standing just inside the gate with her arms around a shaggy skewbald's neck. "Good morning, darling Stewball," Lisa heard her say. She walked over to Emily and Carole.

"After everything I've heard about Stewball," Emily said, "frankly, I expected him to look a little more spectacular than this! This is a movie-star horse?" When The Saddle Club's friend Skye Ransom had filmed a movie at the Bar None, Stewball had been used as a stunt horse.

"Only because he takes such good direction," Lisa said. "We had to dye his coat so that he would match this gorgeous, brainless horse they brought in. They used the gorgeous horse for close-ups."

"Stewball's a fabulous cow horse," Carole added. "He can cut a cow out of a herd like nobody's business. In fact, that's really the reason Stevie didn't buy him. She was going to, but it would have meant taking him away from the one thing he loves and does well. He wasn't cut out to be an English horse."

"He's still gorgeous," Stevie said hotly, coming toward them leading Stewball. "Emily, I heard what you just said about my darling not looking spectacular. All I can say is, if we were having a beauty contest, I'm not sure Stewball would do worse than P.C."

Emily laughed. "Pretty is as pretty does. I've said that a hundred times myself. Don't get your dander up, Stevie. I'll say he's gorgeous if you want me to."

"You'll say he's gorgeous on your own, once you see me ride him," Stevie said. "He's a horse and a half."

Kate led two horses over, Spot for Emily and a pretty red roan named Berry for Carole.

Carole gave Berry a hug. "We always ride the same horses when we're here," she explained to Emily.

Finally Kate brought out Lisa's bay mare, Chocolate, and her own Moonglow. Before long they were all ready to ride. They had agreed that Emily should have just a little more practice in the Western saddle before they hit the trails, so they all warmed up in the empty side paddock.

After trotting and loping Tex a few times around the arena, John showed Lisa and the others why Tex's hindquarters were so heavily muscled. "Watch this!" He loped Tex three-quarters of the way down the side of the fence, then sat back and gave an invisible command. Instantly, Tex seemed to sit down. His hindquarters dropped and locked; he left skid marks ten feet long as he slid to a stop.

The Saddle Club cheered. "He's really getting good!" Carole said. "He's really listening to you."

John inspected the skid marks with a proud smile. "That wasn't too bad," he admitted. "See, he stopped nice and straight."

"That was amazing," Emily said. "What was that?"

"It's a reining move with a very complicated, technical name," John explained with a grin. "We call it a stop. The longer the skid, the better."

"I want to learn how," Emily declared. "Does Spot do it?"

John shook his head. "Later in the week, I'll start to teach you both."

"Great!" Emily loped Spot up the arena and back. She sat up, and Spot came to an obedient, but normal, halt. "Don't forget," she said to John.

"I won't." Next he demonstrated a rollback. He galloped Tex down the fence line, then all in one motion turned him around and galloped straight back. He did large fast circles dropping into slow small ones, he changed leads at a gallop, and he spun in circles. The girls applauded.

"If we had a cow, I could show off Stewball's cutting skills," Stevie told Emily.

"I'll get some," John volunteered. He rode out the gate, and in a few minutes he was back, herding three young calves in front of Tex. The calves trotted into the ring and stood in a confused-looking miniature herd.

"We had them up by the barn to get vaccinated," Kate explained. "Go for the one with the white ear, Stevie."

Stevie pointed Stewball at the calf with the white ear. Then, to make a point, she tucked her reins loosely under her knee and crossed her arms over her chest. While Stevie sat motionless in the saddle, Stewball moved in on the calf. He dodged right, left, and left again, and suddenly the calf was trotting in front of him, away from the other two.

"Wow," Emily said. "I've never seen anything like that. He does it entirely on his own, doesn't he?"

Stevie picked up the reins and gave Stewball a hug. "He certainly does. All you have to do is stay out of his way. But he's not an autopilot horse, except when there are cows around."

"You show us something, Kate," Carole asked. She gave Berry's neck a warm pat. Part of what she always looked forward to about the Bar None was seeing how Kate and John trained the horses. Carole liked riding English best because she loved to jump, but she was always interested in learning new things. Someday she'd like to try her hand at reining, too.

"Moonglow doesn't do reining moves as well as Tex," Kate said, "and she doesn't cut as well as Stewball. But here's one thing she does better than either of them. Move away from that barrel, Emily." Emily jogged Spot away from one of the three barrels in the middle of the ring.

"Hi-yahiiyi-yah!" Kate shouted to Moonglow, and the mare burst forward into a gallop. When they were even with the first barrel, Kate pivoted Moonglow tight around it. She galloped toward the second, spun around it, then spun around the third and galloped back toward the others. "Whoa," Kate said softly, and Moonglow dropped back to a walk.

"So *that's* what those barrels are for," Emily said.

37

"Yep." Kate was slightly out of breath. "We're going to barrel race at some horse shows this fall." She settled her cowboy hat more firmly on her head. "This has been fun, but hadn't we better get going? Emily, you look like you were born in that saddle. Let's hit the trails."

Jogging Stewball around the clumps of sagebrush that dotted the ranch landscape felt like heaven on earth to Stevie. She couldn't believe how lucky she was. In front of her, Emily swayed slightly in the saddle in time to Spot's long-reaching walk. Behind her, Carole hummed contentedly beneath her breath. Lisa, John, and Kate rode ahead. Most of the people she most enjoyed riding with were right here, around her, under this deep-blue bowl-shaped sky. Stevie's heart soared.

"Hey, Stevie, remember the time we were camp counselors out here?" Carole's voice cut into Stevie's reverie.

"Ugh—don't remind me." A few years ago, Eli Grimes, one of the Bar None's former wranglers, had invited The Saddle Club to be junior counselors at a camp he was running. It had been a difficult week, to say the least. "At least *I* didn't fall off leading a trail ride," Stevie said.

Carole laughed. "Don't remind me."

Emily twisted in the saddle. "You fell off? Carole, I didn't think you ever fell off."

Carole rolled her eyes. "Please. I'd be the only rider ever who hadn't. But it wasn't much fun getting dumped in front of a bunch of sniggering little brats, I'll tell you. They were all convinced they could ride better than me."

The trail widened, so Carole and Stevie came up beside Emily. Emily waved her crop in the air. "You were right—no fences," she said. "This is the most beautiful place I've ever been. I love it here."

"We do, too," Stevie said. "That camp was the only bad week we've ever had here. Part of that was our fault, but part was just bad luck."

"And part was because we had to work the whole time," Carole said. "I don't mind work in general, but I have to admit, it's a lot more fun to just ride."

"A whole week of riding," Emily said. "This is wonderful." The trail they had been on widened further into open prairie. Lisa, Kate, and John waited for them to catch up, and they all rode on together. "You know," Emily continued, "when I was a little girl, I used to daydream about being in a place like this. Even before I knew how to ride, I pictured myself on a galloping pony, bareback, with the wind blowing and the whole prairie stretched out before us. We could run forever and never get to the end." She gave a self-conscious laugh. "Silly, isn't it?"

"Not at all," Kate declared. "And it's a daydream that can come true. Spot's a horse, not a pony, and I think you'd do better to keep the saddle on him for now, but we've got the prairie and the wind, and we can certainly gallop. Want to?"

"You bet!"

Kate launched Moonglow into a gallop and Emily sent Spot right behind. The others followed, laughing. Carole bent over Berry's neck, feeling the mare's strides swallow the ground. Thoroughbreds were the fastest horses over long distances, but nothing could beat a quarter horse in the first quarter mile. Berry caught Moonglow and passed her. Tex streaked ahead of even Berry, and Chocolate surged right on Berry's heels.

John's arm went up to signal to the others that he was slowing down. One by one, they brought their panting horses to a walk. Emily's face glowed. "That was fabulous!" she said. "Thank you, Kate, thank you!"

Kate grinned. "You're welcome. But remember, this is only the first morning. We'll have lots of gallops this week. What now? Do we keep going, or head back?"

"I hate to say this," Stevie said, "but I'm starving."

"I second that," Emily said.

Kate turned Moonglow. "Back it is. But really, what were we thinking? Next time we'll bring food." Then she said to Emily, "Something about the prairie makes people hungry. You should see how much some of the ranch guests eat."

"I hope nobody's keeping track of what I eat," Stevie said, in mock alarm.

"Oh, we have been," John said with a straight face. "But the deal is, as long as you still eat less than Stewball, we won't charge you for groceries." He turned to Lisa. "I have to tell you, though, she's getting pretty close. I've been encouraging old Stewball to eat up, but Stevie may be in trouble soon." They all roared. "Hey, there's my dad waving. I'd better go." John said good-bye to all of them, then loped across the prairie to where his father stood next to a pickup truck loaded with hay.

"Does he always work so hard?" Emily asked.

"Always," Kate confirmed. "John's a born rancher. We're lucky to have him and his father here."

As they approached the ranch buildings, they saw a large car pull up and stop outside the house. "That must be Monica," Kate said. She urged Moonglow into a faster walk. "Come on, let's go say hello."

By the time they were close, a man and a woman had gotten out. The man was unloading suitcases from the back, while the woman leaned over an open back door, speaking to someone inside. "Hello, Mr. and Mrs. Hopkins," Kate called cheerily.

Both adults jumped, as though startled, and when they turned toward Kate, both looked worried. In fact, thought Lisa, they looked as though they wished they hadn't come. They greeted Kate in muted voices, and Lisa thought it looked as if they were making a big effort to smile.

"I'm glad you're back," Kate said. "Hi, Monica!"

The figure in the car made no response. Lisa

and Carole exchanged glances. Lisa felt awkward. Mr. Hopkins pulled a pair of metal crutches, like Emily's, out of the trunk of the car. He handed them to his wife. "Here, darling," Mrs. Hopkins said, handing them to the girl in the car. "No, not—oh dear. Try it this way—"

"Mother, that hurts! Stop it!" The girl's voice was strident.

"Oh, I'm sorry. Look who's here, darling, it's Kate. And some other visitors."

"Great," said Monica. "Spectators. Just what I need." She didn't say it loudly, but the wind carried her words back to Lisa, who flinched. They should have given Monica a chance to meet them on her own terms. But then, Kate would have ridden up to greet them if Monica hadn't been hurt, so she should do the same thing now—shouldn't she?

Monica stood up, supporting herself on the crutches. She had long red hair and an angry expression. Just like them, she was wearing a cowboy hat, T-shirt, and jeans, but the right leg of her jeans had been neatly folded and pinned under so that it wouldn't dangle where her leg should have been.

"Hi, Monica," Kate said, in a slightly strained tone.

Monica glanced briefly at Kate, then looked away. "Hi."

Kate introduced her friends to Mr. and Mrs. Hopkins and to Monica. "They'll be staying here almost as long as you will be," she said. Monica didn't respond.

Emily spoke up. "You know," she said to Monica, "you ought to do what we did when we got here—let the grown-ups take the luggage, and get on a horse as quick as you can! We'll get a snack and wait for you, and we can all ride together."

Monica scowled at Emily. "I can't do that," she said rudely.

Emily flushed but remained polite. "Why not? We don't mind waiting."

Monica's face turned red. She looked as if she didn't know whether to cry or to spit at Emily. "I should think it would be obvious why not," she said. "People with one leg don't ride horses." She turned her back on Emily and hopped toward the car.

"Sure they do," said Emily.

Monica turned back, scowling, to say something over her shoulder. Lisa was sure it would have been something rude, but they never got to hear it. Monica tripped over the curb and fell in a tangle of crutches. Her parents rushed forward.

"Oh dear! Are you hurt?" her mother asked.

"No!" Monica threw a crutch sideways. She pounded her fist in the dirt. Tears streamed down her face. "This is stupid!" she yelled. "You were right—we should never have come here! I can't do this! I can't do anything anymore!"

MR. AND MRS. Hopkins huddled over their daughter. After her angry outburst, Monica fell silent; she seemed to be trying to contain her tears. Mrs. Hopkins put her arms around her daughter's shoulders while Mr. Hopkins retrieved the crutch that she'd thrown out of reach.

"I'm sorry I yelled," she muttered, as they helped her stand. "Yelling doesn't change things. I know that." Her face was red and tear-streaked.

"I know, dear," said her mother. "It's all right. I'm sorry, too—I never thought it was a good idea to come here."

"We can go straight home," said her father.

Monica looked at the ground. She still hadn't looked at The Saddle Club or Kate or Emily, and she seemed very embarrassed and upset. "No. I want to stay. We always come to the Bar None." She began to slowly hitch herself toward the ranch house. She didn't look back, not even at Kate, her friend. Her parents followed, hovering around her like a pair of butterflies.

"Well," Kate said, with a soft sigh, when the Hopkinses had gone inside, "that was awful!"

"I feel terrible," Lisa agreed. "Did we say something we shouldn't have?"

Emily turned Spot back toward the stable. "I'm sorry if I shouldn't have asked her to ride. I thought it might be easier on her to try it right away."

Kate shook her head. "No, I think asking her was okay. I don't think we said or did anything wrong." She fiddled with the end of her reins. "I'm just not sure anything we could have said would have been right. This is so hard."

In somewhat depressed silence, they took their horses back to the stable and began to unsaddle.

Before they were finished, the dinner bell rang for lunch.

"Already!" Stevie said. "No wonder we're so hungry! It's later than I thought."

"No wonder I'm so sore," Emily said, as she hung Spot's bridle in the tack room. "We rode a long time."

The others looked at her with concern. "You're sore?" Carole asked.

"Sure. Aren't you?"

Carole thought about it. "I guess so. But just a little, in my legs and seat. Everyday ride-a-lot sore."

Emily shook her head playfully. "Me too. Did you think maybe I had some kind of special soreness?"

Stevie snorted and Carole rolled her eyes. "You could have, for all I know," Carole said. "You have to tell us if we're pushing you too hard, Emily. We don't forget that you haven't done anything like this before."

"I know," Emily said, as they began to walk toward the ranch house. "But you don't remember it every single second of the day, either, and I appreciate that. Don't worry. I'm just regular old saddle sore, and I'm glad of it. It means I'm get-

48

ting some good exercise, and, more importantly, it means I spent the entire morning on a horse!"

"Hear, hear!" cried Stevie. "Hooray for horses! Hooray for saddles! Hooray for being saddle sore!"

"I wouldn't go that far," protested Lisa.

"Oh, come now," said Stevie. "Surely, for the glory of spending a morning amidst the hills and scrubs, amidst the open prairie—"

"Amidst the amber waves of grain—" Carole teased.

Kate began to hum "God Bless America."

Stevie continued, ignoring them. "—surely, for the delight of being one in spirit with these wonderful four-footed creatures here on this glorious ranch—"

"Are you talking about the horses?" Lisa asked.

"Surely," Stevie said loudly, "a little momentary discomfort to the posterior regions is something we can all willingly endure!"

"Well, of course," Emily said. "I said so all along."

They went into the ranch house and sat down. "Neither of the honeymoon couples has come for breakfast yet," Mrs. Devine informed them, as she set a plate of barbecue sandwiches in front of them. "Kate, after lunch I want you to take some baskets of food to their bunkhouses. Just leave them on the porches for them. After I run you into town, I have some errands to do, so I won't be around to feed them until dinnertime."

Kate's mouth dropped open. "How could I forget!"

"Forget what?" Carole asked.

"Christine's dog show! I mean," Kate amended, "I didn't forget I had to help her, I just forgot to tell you guys about it. I've had so many things to tell you!"

"Christine is another one of our friends out here," Lisa explained to Emily. "She lives just on the other side of the ranch, and she usually rides with us a lot. She's got a horse named Arrow and a dog named Dude."

"She's been training Dude for dog obedience trials," Kate said. "Have you seen those? They're miniature obstacle courses, with jumps and ramps and all sorts of things. The fastest dog wins."

"I saw some once at a fair," Emily said. "It was hilarious."

"So I've been helping Christine with Dude, and I promised I'd come to the trials, to assist her—sort of like being a groom at a horse show. This is just a little event, like a practice. I know Christine would love to have you come, but I don't think she'll care if you don't. I mean, if you come you wouldn't be able to ride this afternoon."

"Not ride!" Emily spooned some coleslaw onto her plate. "I thought you guys rode all the time!" Remembering how funny the other dog trials had been, she almost wished she were going to see Dude perform. Almost.

Stevie passed Lisa the bowl of chips. She looked up at her friend and knew Lisa was thinking the exact same thing she was. It would be great to see Christine and Dude, but Emily couldn't ride by herself on the trails. She would have to go to the dog trials, too—and she was so excited about riding. They glanced across the table at Carole, who also seemed to be sharing their thoughts.

"Not ride!" Stevie said. "We couldn't not ride!"

"Tell Christine good luck for us, please, Kate," Lisa said, "but we were planning to spend the afternoon in the saddle."

51

Kate smiled. "She'll be less nervous without an audience, anyway," she said. "I know she'll understand."

"Ask her to come back and ride with us," Carole said. "She needs to meet Emily."

Kate agreed readily. "Don't show Emily all the good spots until I get back."

"How could we?" Stevie asked. "We can't ride fast enough to see all the good spots in one afternoon."

THE SADDLE CLUB and Emily offered to clean up the kitchen so that Kate and her mother could leave. Stevie cleared the table, Emily started filling the dishwasher, and Carole and Lisa began to put the extra food away. Suddenly a thought occurred to Lisa. "They didn't eat!" she said.

"The honeymoon couples? Kate remembered to put their baskets out," Carole replied.

"No, Monica and her parents. They didn't come to lunch. Should we make them a basket, too?"

Carole paused from pouring leftover chips back into their bag. "I don't know. They must have heard the lunch bell. Wouldn't they have come by now?"

"Maybe they aren't hungry," Emily suggested. "Maybe they had lunch in the car on the way here."

"Or maybe they're just getting settled," Lisa said. "My mother always likes to unpack before she does anything."

"Since they've been here before, they'll know where they can get food if they're hungry," Carole said. "I guess they probably don't need a basket. What do you think the chances are that Monica will come riding with us this afternoon?"

"Slim," Lisa said. She grabbed a wet cloth and wiped the countertop down. "She doesn't think she can do it, remember?"

"She might change her mind and want to try," Emily said. They all agreed that this was possible.

When they were finished with the kitchen, they went outside and looked at the long row of bunkhouses. "That's Monica's, the third one down," Lisa said, pointing. "I saw Colonel Devine and Mr. Hopkins carrying their luggage in."

Carole bit her lip. "Do you think we should go ask Monica to ride?" she asked. She hated to think of Monica's being left out, but on the other hand the girl hadn't acted very friendly, and she didn't know them at all. Probably she wouldn't come with them.

Stevie looked at the quiet bunkhouse and shook her head. "Let's give her until tomorrow. We'll ask her then." They all agreed.

They started to walk back to the barn, but before they were halfway there, Colonel Devine came out of one of the outbuildings and began to walk alongside them. "Do you all have specific plans for this afternoon?" he asked.

"We're riding," said Stevie.

He laughed. "I guessed that. I mean, do you have somewhere special you're planning on riding?"

"Everywhere seems special here," Carole said. "But no, we're saving all the extraspecial rides for when Kate and Christine can be with us."

Colonel Devine grinned. "Then maybe, since Kate isn't here, you'd spend the afternoon with me. I've got a few new trails to show you."

"New trails? Cool!" said Stevie.

Inside the barn, John proudly showed off the narrow shelves he'd built into the aisle. He'd added one near every pair of cross-ties, and he'd put them on hinges so that they could fold against with the wall when not in use. "I rounded the corners, too," he said, "so that if a horse bumps into one, it won't get scratched."

Emily examined the shelves with pleasure. "Gosh, we should have you come to Free Rein!" she said. "These are fancy!"

"Wait until you see the rest of our handiwork," Colonel Devine said. He saddled up a big Appaloosa gelding for himself, and before long they were all ready to ride.

"Here we go," Colonel Devine said, leading the way at a swinging walk. He rode behind the barn and followed the paddock fence for a little while. Where the fence ended a small patch of scrub and a stand of pine trees began. The land rolled away toward a wide stream.

"This is pretty!" Carole exclaimed. "I didn't know this was here."

"It's so close to the ranch house, it's easy to overlook," Colonel Devine replied. "Now, do you see my markers?" He pointed to a row of small, widely separated wooden signs, bearing the numbers 1 through 6. "Which one first, ladies?"

"Begin at the beginning, I guess." Lisa was mystified. "Are these riding trails?" Now that she looked, she could see several wide paths leading

56

into the woods and brush. The Bar None was so big that the horses rarely wore trails in the earth even along the most popular rides. There was simply too much grass. But these looked as if they were cut on purpose.

"Trail Number One it is." Colonel Devine rode toward it. "We can fit three abreast on these trails. Emily, you come up here and ride beside me. I'll want your opinions."

Emily rode forward with a smile on her face. "You made these trails, didn't you?"

He grinned back. "You're a fine rider," he said, "and I know you can handle anything on this ranch. But as you know, our ranch has always welcomed beginner riders. On a quiet, well-trained horse, with proper supervision and if they take it slow, most beginners can ride over most of our land, too. But if you have a beginner rider who's also disabled—"

"A lot of the riders at Free Rein are more disabled than me," Emily said, nodding her head understandingly. "Some of the people who use wheelchairs all the time probably won't ever be able to ride safely without having someone lead their horse or walk beside it to make sure they don't fall."

57

"Leaders and sidewalkers," Colonel Devine said. "I know all about it. See? I've been doing a lot of research.

"I don't want to limit our guests to just riding in the paddocks, no matter what their circumstances. I want them to be able to enjoy the land. That's why I developed these trails, and that's why they're so wide—so that the leaders and sidewalkers would have enough room."

Emily looked around. Trail Number One was a simple walk through pine trees. Sunlight filtered coolly through the branches, and the air smelled sharp. Birds twittered. They could hear the gurgling of the nearby stream. The path was wide, as Colonel Devine had said; it was also smooth and flat, with none of the rocks or bumps she'd noticed elsewhere. "I think you were really smart," she said. "People will love it here."

"I hope so," he replied. "Guests only come back a second time if they've enjoyed the first. Now, as we ride along, try to imagine that some of the other people from Free Rein are here. Tell me if you think I should change anything. Okay?"

"Okay," Emily promised. She closed her eyes briefly. The wind blew against her face. The pine scent seemed sharper. "Even the blind people will love it," she said.

"Blind riders?" Colonel Devine sounded surprised.

"Sure," Emily said. "We've got tons of them at Free Rein. I know one girl who jumps."

"How could she?"

Emily shrugged. "Her horse can see."

They rounded a bend and Emily saw to her surprise that they were back at the barn.

"Trail Number One is the shortest," Colonel Devine explained, as they waited for The Saddle Club, who had fallen a little behind. "It's only half a mile long. I figured that might be enough for some of the walkers. I end all the trails at the barn, too, to make things easier on everyone. Ready for Trail Number Two?"

Each trail was a little different, and they were progressively longer; Trail Number Six lasted nearly three miles and included two shallow stream crossings. Colonel Devine had graded the crossings and added sand to keep them smooth. "What about the walkers here?" Emily asked, as Spot splashed across. "Will they have to get their feet wet?"

"We'll tell them to wear waterproof boots for

Number Six," Colonel Devine replied. "Foot-bridges would just wash out in the spring floods. A crossing is easier for us to maintain."

Since they stayed at a quiet walk, riding the six trails took up the entire afternoon. Back at the barn, Colonel Devine had one final question for Emily. "Mr. Brightstar and I have been talking, and we could fence in Trail Number One," he said. "If we ran a rail fence down both sides—"

"No," Emily cut in firmly. She leaned against Spot, gathering her strength before sliding his heavy saddle off. "No fences."

"But I thought—"

"No fences," Emily persisted. "Not here."

Colonel Devine grinned. "All right, then."

Mr. Brightstar came up to speak to Colonel Devine, and John followed and offered to take care of the horse. Colonel Devine agreed, and the two men went off, talking urgently.

"There's a problem with the water pump in the calf pasture," John explained to Emily. He turned toward her just in time to see her nearly drop Spot's saddle in the aisle. He grabbed it quickly. "Whoa, Emily! What's wrong?"

Emily started to lose her balance. She caught herself and sat down on the hay bale that was still in the aisle. "I guess I'm tired," she said. "My legs aren't cooperating, and I'm even having trouble straightening my arms."

John bent forward. "Are you okay?" he asked. "Lisa!" He motioned her over. Lisa and the rest of The Saddle Club came quickly.

"What's wrong?" Lisa asked.

"I'm just tired," Emily said. "I always have a little more trouble when I'm tired. Please, it's no big deal, I promise. Only, would one of you mind putting Spot's saddle away for me? I can handle everything else."

"Sure." Stevie took the saddle from John and swung it onto her hip. "These things are a lot heavier than English saddles, anyway."

"Is there anything else we can do?" Carole asked. Lisa went back to Chocolate's side, but Carole stayed near Emily, just in case. Emily did look tired, and the tiredness seemed to be making the muscles in her arms and legs more tense than usual.

"No," Emily said. "I'm fine, I promise. A hot bath is all I need. And dinner. I'm starving."

"Me too. Whenever we ride this much, we always get this hungry. Colonel Devine said we were having chicken and noodles."

"Great!" Emily stood and started to brush Spot off. Carole returned to Berry. John finished taking care of Colonel Devine's horse and put Spot out in the pasture for Emily. Just as they finished tidying the barn, the supper bell rang.

On the way to the ranch house, Emily walked much more slowly than usual. Her friends kept pace with her. Lisa tried not to show how anxious she felt. What if all that riding had done Emily some harm?

"Lisa," Emily said, as if she could read her thoughts, "if you don't stop hovering over me I'm going to hit you with my crutch. Think about it. You guys have seen me this tired before—it's when I usually resort to using my wheelchair." She tripped and fell but got up quickly.

"I could get your wheelchair," Stevie volunteered. "It would only take a second."

Emily continued forward. "For a two-minute walk to the ranch house? Please, don't be silly." She fell again. "Okay," she said as she stood back up, "so it's becoming a two-hour walk to the ranch house. I *still* don't want my wheelchair. I want to let it get all dusty and cobwebby under my bunk. I'm not going to use it at all this week."

Lisa could see how determined Emily was. "We want to do what's best for you," she said.

"What's best for me is a big plate of chicken and noodles. That, and no wheelchair. See, Stevie?" she added, as she started up the ramp to the ranch house porch. "It didn't take me two hours after all."

"You're the one who said it would," Stevie retorted. "I never thought it would take you longer than an hour and a half."

Emily laughed. "I'm glad to be around people who have faith in me."

Carole opened the door to the house. "We're just glad to be around you," she said.

Inside, only seven places were set for dinner. As the girls sat down, Kate and Mrs. Devine came out of the kitchen with big platters of chicken and noodles and steamed vegetables. Carole jumped up to help them bring out rolls and fruit salad.

"Where is everybody?" Stevie asked.

Kate and Mrs. Devine looked at each other. "Well, the honeymooners are taking some more moonlight rides," Mrs. Devine said. Colonel Devine came in and sat down, and they all started eating.

"Monica won't come to dinner," Kate added

sadly. "Her mom came and got some food to take back to their bunkhouse."

"She said Monica was tired from the trip," Mrs. Devine explained, putting a sympathetic arm around Kate's shoulder.

"She also said Monica was embarrassed," Kate said, sounding disappointed and hurt. "She came up to Mom and whispered, 'Monica doesn't want the girls to see her with, you know, one leg.' As if we cared about that!"

"Plus, we've already seen her with, 'you know, one leg,' " Stevie said. "That doesn't make sense. She's not likely to grow a new leg while she's here, so unless she plans on staying inside her bunkhouse the whole time, we're going to see her with one leg."

"I know," Kate said gloomily. "I wish—I mean, we *were* friends. Why would she be embarrassed to be around me?"

"Don't be hard on her," Carole said gently. "Everything's still so new for her that it's got to be difficult. This is only her first night here, and she doesn't know us at all. No wonder she's feeling shy. Kate, I'm sure she still counts you as a friend—she's just having a hard time right now."

"Anyone would be," Lisa said. She couldn't

imagine the adjustment it would take. "I'm sure she'll feel better by the end of the week."

"Unfortunately," Mrs. Devine said, as she passed the vegetables to Stevie, "I don't think the Hopkinses are going to stay here that long."

"Mom!" Kate said. "They made reservations for a week!"

"Monica's miserable," Mrs. Devine replied. "She's so unhappy that they really regret coming. Mrs. Hopkins told me she and her husband never thought it was a good idea. Monica's been crying all afternoon. She can't ride, she says, and that's all she ever did when they came here before."

"I suppose seeing us all on horseback didn't help," Kate said gloomily. She set her fork down and pushed the plate away.

"How ever Monica's feeling right now, it's not your fault," her father told her sternly. "You just go on being her friend as best you can, and let her work out her problems." He spoke to his wife. "Monica should be able to ride, though, shouldn't she? I can't think of a reason why she shouldn't. She can start on our new trails, if she feels unsteady—but she was such a good rider, I'm sure she'll be able to compensate."

Emily spoke up. "Her seat'll feel the same, and she'll be able to use the reins just as well. Did she ever ride English?"

Kate shook her head. "Just Western. She used to barrel race sometimes."

"She'll have to get used to carrying a crop, to substitute for leg signals, but that won't be too hard," Emily continued. "I think once she's on a horse she'll do okay. It's getting her on one that might be the problem."

Stevie took a roll and tore it into pieces. She spread butter on each piece. "Maybe we could make a plan," she said excitedly. "We can trick her into riding. Maybe Kate can ride Moonglow over to the Hopkinses' bunkhouse, and then she can fall off and pretend to be injured. The only way Monica will be able to get help fast enough is to hop on Moonglow and gallop—"

"Forget it," Carole said. "That'll never work. In the first place, the bunkhouse is only fifty yards from here. Kate could yell and someone would hear her. In the second place, Monica's mom and dad are right there with her, so one of them would do all the rescuing, anyway."

"Okay," said Stevie, undaunted. She stuffed

two pieces of roll into her mouth and chewed hard, thinking. "Okay, how about this. We lure Monica out—"

"Forget that, too," Emily said. "We can't make her ride. We can't *make* her do anything. She has to come to terms with being disabled on her own. We can encourage her, but we can't force her. The last thing she needs, Stevie, is one of your schemes. Monica needs to decide to ride on her own."

Stevie sighed. "I guess you're right."

"I know I am," Emily said.

Colonel Devine changed the subject, telling Kate and his wife all about that afternoon's ride. "I think they liked our trails," he said proudly.

"Did you?" Kate grinned. "I hope so. I helped lay them out, you know, and John and I hauled brush away until we thought we'd die from over-work and exhaustion."

"They're fantastic," Emily said. "Everybody at Free Rein would love to ride somewhere this beautiful."

"Emily had a few good ideas," Colonel Devine continued. "She thought we should put benches halfway through the longer trails, so the leaders would have a place to sit down and rest. And she thought we ought to cut down that low branch you warned me about, Kate."

"I told you so," Kate replied.

"Emily's been thinking hard all day," Stevie said with a grin. "The rest of us, we're not thinking about anything except where to ride next, and what we can eat when we're finished riding."

"Tomorrow we're going to combine them," Lisa said. "We'll take a picnic breakfast, if that's okay."

"Sure," Mrs. Devine agreed. "I'm already doing that for the honeymooners."

Emily dropped her fork with a clatter. "Sorry," she said with a blush. "I told The Saddle Club in the barn, I'm a little tired tonight."

"Hope I didn't make you think too hard today," Colonel Devine said, looking at her closely. "Or ride too hard, for that matter."

Emily smiled. "No—I would have been happy to ride longer. And I'm not thinking all that hard, either. Plus, this afternoon was a double pleasure for me. I got to ride, and I got to imagine all the people who would be able to ride here in the future. It was wonderful."

"I would have liked to have gone with you," Kate said. "The dog show was fun, though. Dude got third place in his division, and Christine says hello to all of you. She'll come over sometime tomorrow."

"I can't believe we forgot to ask you about the dog show!" Carole said. "I guess we were too busy riding."

"One-track minds," Kate teased.

"You know us too well," Carole retorted.

"Carole especially," Stevie said. "The rest of us do sometimes think about, oh, books or movies or boys once in a while. I believe Lisa sometimes thinks about clothes. But with Carole it's horses, horses, riding, and then horses."

Frank Devine spooned his third helping of chicken and noodles onto his plate. "Well, I'm going to go look at horses tomorrow," he said. "I'm spending the day at a livestock auction. With luck I'll get a few more horses for the ranch herd, and maybe even some cattle so we'll have something for the horses to round up. It's not riding, but you girls are welcome to come with me if you'd like."

"Sounds interesting," Stevie said. "The only problem is what you just said: It's not riding."

"Not riding!" Emily exclaimed. "We can't spend a whole day not riding!"

"Of course not," Carole chimed in. Privately she thought that a horse auction might be interesting—but if both Emily and Stevie wanted to stay at the ranch and ride, she would stay with them. The Saddle Club had to stick together.

"We're like the three musketeers," Lisa said. "Only in this case it's four musketeers. Anyway, all for one and one for all. I vote for riding. Kate?"

Kate was laughing. "Far be it from me to disagree with you all," she said. "I've been to horse auctions before, and I'm sure I'll go to plenty more. If you want to ride, I'll ride with you. So that makes it five musketeers."

After dinner, The Saddle Club and Emily walked back to the bunkhouse. Emily went straight into the bathroom to take a hot bath. Lisa lay down on her bunk. "Phew! I'm tired, too!"

Stevie pulled off her cowboy boots and massaged her toes. "I wouldn't know why," she said.

"Maybe it had something to do with the three brownies I ate for dessert," Lisa suggested. "Sometimes I think my stomach gets so full it makes my eyes shut." She closed her eyes.

"I think Stevie's boots are making my eyes water," Carole said. "Stevie, they stink! Can't you stick them outside?"

"Geez," Stevie grumbled, as she got up and put her boots on the porch. "This is the Wild West. We're supposed to be roughing it."

"Not that rough," Lisa said. "The boots are outside, but the smell is still here. Could it be your socks?"

"Picky, picky," Stevie said. "As a matter of fact, I seem to have forgotten extra socks. These are my only pair."

Lisa rolled over and pulled her duffel bag out from under the bunk. She extracted a pair of socks and threw them at Stevie. "Here."

"Here." Carole did the same thing. "When Emily comes out, ask her for a pair, too. Or Kate. Don't wear the same socks over again, please."

"I had no idea you ladies were so dainty," Stevie said. She went back outside and hung the offending socks on the porch rail.

"That ought to keep us safe from raccoons, coyotes, and bears," Lisa said to Carole. "No wild animal could get past those socks." Carole roared.

"What's so funny?" Emily called through the bathroom door.

"We'll tell you when you get out," Lisa called back. "Only don't drain your bathwater. Stevie needs to rinse her feet."

"Lisa," Carole said suddenly, sitting down on the edge of her friend's bunk, "do you think anything could stop you from riding?"

Lisa opened her eyes. "You mean like an accident or something? Like Monica's?"

"Well, yes," Carole paused. "I remember when Cobalt died, for a little while I didn't think I wanted to ride again." Lisa nodded. She rememberd that time, too. Cobalt had been a horse Carole loved.

"I really did want to ride even then," Carole continued. "I just felt so upset about Cobalt that everything about horses reminded me of him and how much I missed him, and how stupid it was that he had to die. But I think if something happened to me, no matter what it was, I would want to ride. I don't think anything could stop me. If I could be on a horse, I would be."

"I don't think anything could stop you, either," Lisa agreed. "Horses mean so much to you.

I think I would want to ride, too. But maybe Monica feels differently. She sounds like a really active person—motorbiking and all. Maybe she's afraid riding will remind her of all the things she used to be able to do."

"Yeah. Imagine being able to remember how it felt to walk, or run, or kick a ball and not being able to do it anymore," Stevie said.

Kate came in the door with a Scrabble set and a box of brownies under her arm. "Who are you talking about? Monica?"

Lisa nodded. "We were trying to think about how she might feel."

"Which do you think would be worse?" Stevie asked. "To be disabled from the minute you were born, or to become disabled suddenly when you were our age?"

Emily opened the bathroom door.

"I don't know," Kate said. "I think it's worse for Monica this way, but I don't know."

Emily shook her head. "I would give anything if I could run," she said. "Just once. Once, to see how it would feel."

STEVIE WOKE WHEN a beam of sunlight hit her square in the face. She opened her eyes, blinked hard, and sat up. The door of the bunkhouse was open. She could hear Lisa snoring in the bunk below. Across the room, she could see Carole sleeping in the top bunk and Kate with her face buried in her pillow on the cot. Emily's bunk was empty.

Stevie pushed the covers to one side and dropped quietly to the floor. She walked to the door of the cabin. Emily was standing on the porch, leaning against the railing, looking up at the mountains and the bright, early morning sky. Her face was radiant.

"Hi," Stevie said softly.

Emily looked over her shoulder. "Stevie! Good morning. Did you ever see such a beautiful day?"

Stevie grinned and sniffed the air. It smelled like damp earth, dewy meadow grass, and bacon from the ranch house. If she sniffed hard she could even smell a hint of the horses. She couldn't smell her socks at all. The night air must have cured them.

"If you think this is beautiful, wait until you see the sun rise over the hills," she said.

Emily nodded. "Our sunrise ride. I'm looking forward to it." On the last day of every visit to the Bar None, The Saddle Club always took a bareback sunrise ride.

"Have you been awake long?" Stevie asked.

"No." Emily grinned. "I slept well! I hope I didn't keep you guys awake with my snoring."

"You lost the Scrabble game," Stevie informed her. "We made you forfeit your turns after you fell asleep."

"I couldn't help it," Emily protested. "Carole was taking half an hour for her turns."

"That's because she's not happy making regular words. She has to make horse words," Stevie said. "Her triumph last night was *fetlocks*. She got the bonus for using all seven letters, plus we gave her a Saddle Club bonus for the horse word. But it didn't matter. Lisa always wins."

Emily laughed. "The moment she turned my word *play* into *displaying*, I knew I was in trouble," she said in agreement. "I figured I might as well go to sleep. But I'm glad I woke up now. Let's get those sleepyheads up. We don't want to waste the whole morning."

Stevie agreed. "It's time to ride!"

As THEY DRESSED, Kate told them that she was going to go ask Monica to come with them. "I always used to knock on her cabin door for early morning rides," she explained. "She might even be expecting me."

The other girls slipped into the ranch house kitchen and packed their backpacks with biscuits and apples. Carole boiled some water for hot chocolate and filled three thermoses. Before she was finished, Kate walked in, shaking her head sadly. "No one even answered," she said. "No one. I'm sure Monica would have heard me. Maybe she's already down by the barn."

But the barn was empty—even John hadn't started working yet—and Monica was nowhere to be seen. Kate looked a little disappointed, but Lisa thought that there was almost no way Monica would come there early by herself. She hoped Kate would still be able to enjoy the ride.

In fact, it was a perfect morning. As they crested a ridge toward the east end of the ranch, looking up into the sun-touched mountains, they saw another rider coming toward them.

"Christine!" Stevie yelled, and loped Stewball down the slope to meet her. Dude, Christine's dog, frolicked between the horses.

"Hi, everybody." Christine introduced herself to Emily, and Emily to Dude.

"So this is the show dog," Emily said.

"The obedient dog. You bet he is! I was really proud of him yesterday. He's got the commands down pat. Now all he needs to work on is his speed. Watch this!" She rode down the hillside to where a row of sagebrush bushes grew in a line like soldiers. "Dude! Weave!"

To their surprise and delight, Dude wove in

and out through the line of brush, passing one bush on the left side and the next on the right. They cheered. "That's amazing," Lisa said. "I wish I'd seen—well, I wish the trial had been some other time, so we could have been there."

"Yeah," Christine joked, "it's too bad they don't hold them at midnight. That's okay. We'll show you all our tricks out here on the prairie."

"First we need to find a breakfast spot," Carole suggested. "I'm starving."

Christine looked around. "Why not right here?"

Kate shook her head. "Nope."

"Why not? It looks fine."

"Because I can't mount from the ground by myself," Emily explained. "I need something to climb onto, and even then it has to be the right sort of something."

"Oh. Sorry." Christine looked a little embarrassed.

"How could you have known?" Emily asked her. "Besides," she added, with a playful grin at Kate, "if this horse were thoroughly trained, I wouldn't need to worry."

79

Kate and The Saddle Club laughed. Christine, who knew perfectly well what a highly trained horse Spot was, looked confused. Emily explained how P.C. could drop to his knees.

"That's a pretty specialized trick," Kate commented. "I might try to teach Spot someday— but it's asking a lot. Horses don't often lie down in the wild, because they're more vulnerable that way. They'd have to really trust their rider to do it on command."

"P.C. is just naturally brilliant," Emily informed them.

"What does P.C. stand for?" Christine asked.

"Pennsylvania Countryside," Emily replied. "That's where he was born."

The others laughed and again Christine looked confused. "When I asked you what it meant, you told me Pesky Critter," Kate said.

"What P.C. means changes from time to time," Lisa explained.

"P.C. himself, though," said Emily, "stays pretty much the same."

After a careful search, they found the perfect breakfast spot near a small stream. A fallen tree made a decent mounting ramp. Emily dismounted and played with Dude while the others offered the horses water and unpacked breakfast. "You know," Emily said, washing half a biscuit down with a slurp of hot chocolate, "that's another suggestion for your dad, Kate. Maybe he could build some mounting blocks out here."

"That's a great idea," Kate said. "We've got several spots where we often set up picnics or barbecues. I'll tell him."

"And tell your mother she makes good biscuits," Emily said, reaching for another.

After breakfast they rode over some more of the range, and then they rode Christine home. "I promised my mother I'd go into town with her," Christine said. "I'll come back later. Nice to meet you, Emily. See you soon."

"Do you think we should take Emily up to Lookout Point?" Stevie asked. It was the highest spot on the ranch.

"I hate to say this, Stevie, but I'm actually getting a little tired," Lisa said. It was true, but even if it hadn't been, Lisa would have been ready to go back. She didn't want Emily to get worn out again.

"So am I," Emily said. "Do you mind if we see Lookout Point on another ride?"

"Sure," Stevie said. "We've got dozens of rides left."

"Dozens?" Carole asked. "We're only going to be here another three days."

"So if we average four rides a day, that's a dozen," Stevie said.

"Oh, good." Carole sounded relieved.

BACK AT THE RANCH, they weren't quite sure what to do with themselves. John and his father were working, and Monica and the other guests weren't in sight. The girls took thorough care of their horses, then meandered through the empty ranch house. "I guess my mom must have gone to the horse auction with my dad," Kate said. They went out to the porch and sat down in the rocking chairs there.

"Nice porch," Emily said as she rocked.

"Nice prairie," Carole added.

"Yeah."

"Where do you think Monica is?" Carole asked.

"I don't know," Kate said. "Wish she was out here."

"Well," Stevie said, "we should probably get ready to ride again."

"Good idea!" Lisa stood up. "Why don't we go out to the rock where we had Stevie's birthday picnic and eat lunch out there?"

"That's a great idea!" Kate stood up, too, looking enthused. "We've got some picnic tables and benches and straw bales out there now, because we have campfires there all the time. Emily, I'm sure we could improvise a mounting ramp for you."

"Great!"

"I'll call Christine's house and leave her a message, so she knows where to find us," Kate said, heading into the ranch house, "and then I think we should go ask Monica if she wants to come, too. She's had almost a day to reconsider. I bet she's ready to ride now."

"I hope so," Carole said. "She'll feel so much happier once she's on a horse." Carole believed horses always made the tough times in her life easier.

They all went to the front door of the Hopkinses' bunkhouse. Kate knocked loudly. After a long pause, Mrs. Hopkins opened the door just wide enough to stick her head out. She gave them an apologetic smile.

"We'd like to speak to Monica, please," Kate said politely.

Mrs. Hopkins looked dismayed. "I'm sorry, dears," she whispered, "but I don't think she's feeling up to visitors just now."

"We just want to talk to her," Kate said.

"We'd like her to come riding with us," Emily added.

Mrs. Hopkins didn't budge. "She's busy right now. She's in the middle of her physical therapy exercises."

"That's okay," Kate said. "We'll wait."

Mrs. Hopkins gave them a long look. "I think maybe you don't understand," she said, still in a whisper. "Monica's not going to be able to ride anymore. Her father and I think it's too dangerous. And her accident has made her a little depressed. Kate, it's not that she doesn't want to be friends. She's just having a hard time here. We've asked Mr. Brightstar to drive us around the ranch this afternoon in the pickup truck, so she'll be able to enjoy the scenery. But that's all Monica has planned for today. I'll tell her you said hello."

"Wait!" Kate cried, as Mrs. Hopkins clicked the door shut. Kate's shoulders sagged. "She didn't even let us talk to Monica," she said.

Lisa put her arm around Kate. "We'll try again later," she said. "We won't give up." She gently turned her friend around, and they started walking back to the barn.

"Imagine seeing the ranch from the cab of a pickup truck!" Stevie said. "That would be enough to depress anyone."

"It's just so irritating!" Emily exclaimed. "Why do they think horseback riding would be any more dangerous for Monica now than it was before she lost her leg? I mean, accidents can happen to anyone, on any horse."

"Probably they worry about her losing her balance," Lisa said. She didn't understand why Monica's parents were so worried, but she could see why riding would now be more difficult for her. And probably Monica's parents were simply afraid to have her hurt again.

"They can't keep her safe from everything," Emily said, still angry. "She could choke to death on a piece of toast, for Pete's sake. Mr. Brightstar's truck could crash into a ravine. A meteor could fall on her head. Sure her balance will be worse, but so what? You told me she was a good rider. And anyway, if she falls off now, she wouldn't be hurt any worse than if she fell off with two legs."

Emily paused for breath. "I hate it when people treat disabled people like they're made of glass. I mean, okay, kids with stuff like spina bifida have to be really careful—they could get hurt badly by an easy fall—but *all* disabled people don't need to be coddled. I don't need to be coddled, and neither does Monica. She *ought* to ride." She started walking again, her mouth set in a firm line. Lisa could see that her eyes were full of tears.

"Em, Em," she said soothingly. "She will. Everything's still so new for her. Give her time."

Emily drew a shaky breath. "I will. I know. I'm sorry, I don't mean to get upset. It's just one of those things that really gets to me. Her parents shouldn't be setting up rules about what she can't do." They walked into the barn and Emily went straight to Spot's stall. She put her arms around him.

Kate looked thoughtful. "I agree that's what it seemed like Monica's parents were doing," she said, "but I'm not convinced it's true. Remember, I know them better than you guys do. If Monica were insisting that she wanted to ride, they would let her. I bet they're just trying to make her feel like she doesn't have to ride if she doesn't want to."

"I hope so," Emily said.

"I'm sure of it," Kate said. "Monica will ride if she decides she wants to."

"I still think we ought to do something about that," Stevie said. "Last night I thought of this great plan—"

"No!" the rest of them shouted in chorus. "Stevie," Lisa continued, in a practical tone of voice, "you know we can never make you do anything. Why should Monica be any different from you?"

Stevie sighed. "I know you're right, I just want to help her so badly."

"We'll keep asking her to ride," Kate said. "Every day we'll ask her."

THEY BEGAN THEIR ride feeling somewhat subdued, but soon the sheer joy of riding good horses through gorgeous countryside on a beautiful day filled them all. Since they were already hungry, they rode straight for Pulpit Rock and ate their lunches there. Before they were finished, Christine and Dude joined them.

Afterward, Emily said she wanted to gallop again. Kate obligingly led them to an open stretch of prairie.

"Yippee-ki-yi-yay!" Emily shouted, sending Spot forward in a burst of speed.

"Yippee-ki-yi-*what*?" Stevie yelled. She pushed Stewball even with Spot. "What did you say?"

"Yippee-ki-yi-yay!" Emily repeated. "Isn't that what the cowboys say?"

Stevie shook her head. The wind blew her ponytail across her face, and she shook her head again to toss it back. "I've never heard a cowboy say that," she said at last. "Must be a dude thing."

"A *what* thing?" Emily yelled above the sound of galloping hoofbeats.

"Dude!" Stevie shouted, as she pulled Stewball up. Christine's dog came running. Stevie began to laugh. "A *dude* is a city person who tries to act like a cowboy," she explained to Emily, who had slowed Spot and turned him back toward Stewball. "Christine named Dude after us, because she didn't consider us cowboys when we first got here."

"Oh." Emily grinned. "I guess I'm still a dude after all. But by the end of the week, I'll be a cowboy."

"Watch this!" Kate called to them. She gathered Moonglow's reins lightly in her hands, and before they knew it, Moonglow was prancing across the prairie in the light, cadenced movement of a collected dressage trot. Kate sent Moonglow into a half-pass, taking her diagonally into a stand of sagebrush, and then turned and brought her back toward the others in a flashy, athletic extended trot.

"Pretty good," Lisa admitted. "But watch this!" She shot Chocolate into a fast lope, then brought the reins up and back just the way she'd seen John do on their first day. She spun her weight around, and to her delight Chocolate did just what Lisa hoped: a fast rollback. They galloped back.

"Wow, I'm impressed," Carole said. Lisa grinned. She was still the least experienced member of The Saddle Club, and it was fun sometimes to try something the others couldn't already do.

"I know it was rough, not elegant like John's," Lisa said.

"Still, we could tell it was a rollback," Stevie said. "Let me try." Her rollback, though also recognizable, wasn't quite as good as Lisa's. Her version of a stop, however, was impressive. Stewball nearly sat down, and Stevie came perilously close to flying over his ears. She threw her arms around his neck and pushed herself back into the saddle.

"Nice," Lisa said. "But aren't there supposed to be skid marks?"

"Stewball is so cool he doesn't need to skid," Stevie replied, unruffled.

After that Carole made Berry jump a fallen log, and then they all had to follow her. Kate tried to teach Emily dressage collection, but Spot, in his Western bridle, refused to learn. Emily gave up, laughing, and took him for another gallop. Stevie tried to make Stewball cut Lisa's horse out of the crowd. "I'm not a cow!" Lisa protested. "Neither is Chocolate."

Between the noise of the wind and their laughter, they didn't notice Mr. Brightstar's pickup until it was very close to them. "Look, Kate," Carole whispered. They all halted and turned their horses to face the truck. Inside, they could just see Monica sitting between her mother and Mr. Brightstar. They couldn't tell whether or not she was looking at them.

Kate waved, tentatively, and then they all did. Mr. Brightstar stuck his hand out the window to wave back. Monica might have waved, but they couldn't really tell. The truck drove on.

Carole felt an unreasonable surge of guilt. It wasn't her fault Monica wasn't riding, but it seemed a shame that the other girl couldn't enjoy the same fun they were having.

"It was her choice," Kate said, almost bitterly. Carole knew Kate was thinking the same thing. "We asked her to come with us."

"I think I'm ready to go back," Lisa said quietly.

"Me too," Stevie said.

"All of us," said Emily.

"Yeah," said Kate. "This stinks!" Carole couldn't tell exactly what Kate meant, but she thought that whatever it was, she agreed. It stunk that they were riding and Monica was not.

"LOOK!" KATE SAID, as they drew close to the ranch buildings. "There's Dad's trailer! He's home!"

Frank Devine's big stock trailer was parked near the gate of one of the middle-sized outdoor paddocks. The girls quickly turned their horses out for the evening, put their tack away, and went to see if they could help.

"Stand back, girls!" he told them. Mr. Brightstar and John were there already, and as the girls watched they set up tall pieces of plywood to make a chute leading into the pasture. Carole climbed up on the fence to get a closer look. Inside the trailer, the horses moved nervously.

"Okay—careful!" Colonel Devine swung open the back of the trailer. John and Mr. Brightstar reached through the vent windows and unsnapped the lead ropes that tied the first two horses in place. As soon as their heads were free, the horses backed out of the trailer, whirled, and galloped into the pasture. They squealed and tossed their heads.

"You'll have your hands full with this bunch, John," Kate said with a grin.

"Oh yeah? Aren't you helping?" he asked back.

Carole felt a sudden pang of envy for these two, already living full-time around horses. Of course, she did get to spend a lot of time with her own horse, Starlight. Still, to live right next to your horses would be something. She'd love to be able to look out her bedroom window and see Starlight grazing.

The new horses, a buckskin, two pintos, two sorrels, and a bay, milled nervously in the field. Colonel Devine clanged the paddock gate shut, and the girls helped him dismantle the plywood chute.

"They're scared," Emily observed, watching the horses through the fence.

"They've had a confusing day. We'll leave them in there for a few days, give them time to settle, and then start working with them and introducing them to the main herd. They're a good bunch of horses."

"Did you have fun, Dad? Was old Mr. MacGillicutty there?" Kate turned to her friends. "He's this ancient rancher, and he tends to get carried away at auctions. His wife says he can only buy one horse, and he'll buy one, and then he'll start bidding on others. Once she whacked him on the head with a program—" Kate began to laugh.

"I believe Mr. MacGillicutty filled his trailer today," Colonel Devine said with a grin.

"Four horses!" Kate roared. "But I bet they were all 'purty.' He only buys 'purty' ones."

"What does he do with them all?" Carole asked, at the same time as Stevie said, "Just how many horses does he have?"

"A hundred, at least," Kate said, wiping her eyes. "And that's the best part—he doesn't do anything with them. He's got an enormous ranch and the horses seem happy, but all he does is sit out on his front porch and watch them and say,

'Look at all the purty horses!' Sometimes his wife makes him sell some. They are all pretty, too, and it's always easy for him to find buyers."

"Mrs. MacGillicutty wasn't too pleased with him today," Kate's dad added.

"I bet not," said Kate. "What else happened?"

"Oh, let's see. One horse reared up when it was being presented, and the auctioneer said, 'And look what a fine belly this horse has!' "

Carole giggled. She knew that rearing was the most dangerous habit a horse could have, and she also knew that you could rarely, if ever, tell anything about a horse by looking at its belly. But she did wonder how Colonel Devine had decided which horses to buy. His six all looked nice, but temperament was one of the most important things about a horse, and that couldn't be judged on sight. She knew you weren't allowed to ride horses at auctions—so how would you know anything about them? It would be a ferocious gamble. Suddenly, Carole almost wished she'd gone. Colonel Devine could have taught her a lot.

"And the Wilsons bought an adorable elderly pony for their little boys," Colonel Devine continued. "The cattle weren't very impressive, so we didn't buy any, and I had to sit on your mother, Kate, to keep her from bringing home a sheep. The last thing we need is a sheep. Loretta Matthews had another batch of kittens to give away—she always does. That's all. Ate a hot dog, loaded up my horses, came home."

"It sounds like a carnival!" Stevie said. She always thought of auctions as being staid, stiff, formal events, where people in dress clothes silently held up numbered paddles to signify their bids.

"More like a country fair than a carnival," Colonel Devine said. "But we always do have a nice time."

"Gosh—I didn't know it would be like that!" Stevie said. *Maybe,* she thought for a moment, *we should have gone. Only that would have meant no riding.* "But we had a really great time today," she added quickly.

"I wish I'd seen you bid on that sorrel," Emily said, pointing to one of the horses in the paddock. "I like him. I would have liked to have seen how he came into the ring, and how much attention he paid to the crowd."

"Yes—that's a good way of learning something about a horse at auction," Colonel Devine acknowledged. "I like that little sorrel, too. He may be the best of the bunch. And he was cheap, too."

"Really?" Lisa wondered how cheap exactly, but she thought it would be rude to ask. She had begun to realize that she didn't know much about fair prices for horses, and she figured she needed to learn. Someday—someday soon, she hoped—she was going to talk her parents into buying her one. "I guess I would have learned a lot, if we'd gone."

"You'd have learned a lot about pigs and sheep and cattle, too," Kate said. "Also dust and farm equipment. I wish those auctions were more horsey. Dad, we had the best day ever! Two beautiful rides!"

"AREN'T THE HOPKINSES coming?" Kate asked, as they sat down to dinner. Lisa could hear the sadness in her friend's voice.

"I'm afraid not, dear," her mother answered, setting a plate of food on the table. "Mrs. Hopkins asked for carryout again."

Lisa touched Kate's elbow. "We'll ask her to ride with us tomorrow," she reminded her.

"Are you riding tomorrow?" Mrs. Devine asked. She sat down next to Colonel Devine, and they began to eat. "Kate, did you ask them about going to the Wild West Show?"

Kate rolled her eyes. "I forgot! I tell you, all this riding and worrying about Monica has made me forgetful. Right, the Wild West Show is tomorrow, but I wasn't sure you guys would want to go, since you've already seen it twice."

"Seen it?" Stevie said indignantly. "We performed! Stewball and I were the stars of the show!"

"And if I remember correctly," Lisa cut in, "you were so spectacular that you were asked not to perform again."

Amid everyone's laughter, Carole and Kate told Emily about the Wild West Show. "It's a touristy thing," Kate said. "Cowboys, shoot-'em-ups. The Old West like they show it in movies. They do it in town, right in the middle of the day, so that at first tourists don't realize it's a show. The organizers always need local volunteers."

"Once we were playing pioneer women and one of the fake bank robbers threatened Stevie,"

Carole said. "Stewball was tied nearby, and he broke lose and went after the man. It looked like he was defending Stevie, but really he was just trying to get the rock candy the man had in his pocket."

"Stewball," Stevie explained, "loves rock candy."

"His reaction was a little extreme," Kate said. "If we go tomorrow, we'll leave the horses at home. As long as we do that, I'm sure they'll let us be actors again."

Emily thought a Wild West Show sounded fantastic. "I'd love to see it," she said. "It'd be like a movie come to life. And I'd especially like to see you guys perform. I don't think I could, though—I bet they aren't equipped to deal with disabled people on zero notice. Are there steps? Would I have to move fast?"

"Yes, and probably," Kate admitted.

"We won't go," Carole said. "We were planning on riding every day, remember?"

"I'd love to come and watch," Emily persisted. "Maybe Monica would want to come, too. Really, I'd rather—" She cut her words short. It occurred to her suddenly that The Saddle Club had already done the show twice. Probably they didn't want to do it again. "Riding's great, too," she concluded.

"I don't know," Stevie said. "I guess without Stewball it wouldn't be the same, anyway. Lisa?"

Lisa bit her lip. She loved acting; she really loved the Wild West Show. But she tried to put herself in Emily's shoes. How much fun would it be to sit on the sidelines watching your friends run around in bonnets and long dresses? "Let's ride," she said.

Colonel Devine shook his head. "I've heard of horse-crazy, but you all take the cake. Don't you ever get sick of riding? Isn't there anything you'd rather do?"

Carole grinned. "If there is, we haven't found it yet."

"What about Monica?" Emily said. "Should we ask her about the Wild West Show?"

"Oh, come on." Kate sounded bitter. "If she won't even get on a horse, if she won't even come out of her cabin, what are the odds of her going to the Wild West Show?"

Even though she thought that Kate sounded a little harsh, Lisa had to admit that she was right. They didn't need to bother to ask Monica.

"YOU KNOW," KATE said, as they jogged their horses across the beautiful undulating prairie, "I think this is the stalest biscuit I ever ate." She spat out a mouthful of half-chewed biscuit. "Really. It's disgusting."

Behind her The Saddle Club and Emily all threw their biscuits into the dirt. "We're delighted to hear you say that," Stevie said cheerfully. "We were afraid we'd have to be polite and eat them."

"We weren't sure we *could* be that polite," Emily added. The sun had hardly risen, but already they were miles away from the ranch house. This morning they had decided to eat breakfast in the saddle.

"I must have grabbed the biscuits from the wrong jar," Kate said. "Those must have been prehistoric biscuits left here by the indigenous people who were driven south by the last ice age. My mother was probably saving them to send to an archaeologist."

Stevie said, "I'll lend her a stamp."

"Look!" Kate said. "Coyote tracks!"

"Wow!" said Lisa, with a sarcastic laugh. "More coyote tracks! That must mean coyotes live around here." They'd seen approximately three million coyote tracks, and upwards of seventeen thousand coyotes. The animals looked like skinny yellow dogs, and they slinked away from horses. They were, Lisa decided, some of the least attractive animals she'd ever seen.

"I'm hungry," Kate complained, ignoring Lisa. "And I think my mom was going to make omelets for breakfast. And fried potatoes. And sausage."

"Let's have another gallop," Emily suggested.

"Back to the ranch house for food," added Stevie.

"Exactly. But"—Emily grinned at her friends—

"I'm only going in if we can tie these horses to the hitching post so that we can jump right back into the saddle the moment we're through!" She meant it jokingly, but her friends didn't seem to understand that.

"Well, of course," Carole said immediately. The others nodded.

Emily sighed. She had known her friends were horse-crazy, but she'd had no idea they were this horse-crazy. Emily loved riding more than anything else, and it was the highlight of her trip here; on the other hand, some of the other things to do around the ranch sounded like fun. But she wasn't going to spoil The Saddle Club's vacation by saying so.

"KATE," STEVIE SAID, with a satisfied sigh, "this morning's biscuits must have been an aberration. Your mother is the best cook in the world." The omelet had been stupendous, and the potatoes beyond belief.

"I'm telling you," Kate replied, "the biscuits were older than you are. Don't judge Mom by those biscuits, especially since you've eaten her good ones, too. I'm going to go get Monica. Want to come?"

The others immediately got up and followed her out of the ranch house. In the early morning, before their ride, Kate had once again knocked on Monica's door, and once again had gotten no response. "She has to be awake now," Kate said. They knocked on the door.

Mrs. Hopkins answered. "Hello, girls," she said.

"May we speak to Monica?" Kate asked.

"I'll see." She disappeared, and in a moment Monica herself came to the door. Her eyes were rimmed with dark shadows and her face was sad; she looked once at Kate and then down at the ground. She didn't seem to even notice the other girls.

"We're going riding—" Kate began.

"I can't, Kate," Monica interrupted, speaking in a voice so quiet that Lisa had to strain to hear. "I just . . . can't. So don't ask me anymore. Please." She took a step back and shut the door firmly.

Kate looked ready to cry. "I guess I shouldn't have asked," she said.

"No, you're doing the right thing." Lisa gave Kate a hug. "I know you are. Poor Monica! She looks so unhappy."

"Come on, Kate," Stevie urged. "A nice ride will cheer you up, at least."

They rode and then they ate lunch, and then they rode again. "I know we'll never cover this whole ranch in a week, but it sure feels like we have," Carole joked mid-afternoon. She knew for a fact that they'd ridden over all of their usual trails, and, to her surprise, her seat was getting incredibly sore. Maybe her blue jeans were too thin. She remembered a fleece saddle cover she'd seen in a tack catalog. Soft, thick fleece! Now, that would be something worth having.

"You feel that way because all of the sagebrush looks the same," Emily said. She was beginning to think that the Western landscape, despite its eye-opening vistas and amazing beauty, was also really monotonous. Rocks, grass, dirt, and brush. Rocks, grass, dirt, and brush. "You see one sagebrush, you've seen them all. Of course," she added quickly, "this trip has been the best time of my life." And it was true, except there really was too much stupid sagebrush. Emily felt she would pay money to see a nice leafy oak tree.

Stevie caught the slight edge in Emily's voice and sighed. She sure hoped Emily appreciated the magnitude of her own personal sacrifice.

Stevie was sure she would have found a way to take Stewball to the Wild West Show, no matter what the Devines said. She and Stewball were sacrificing their encore shot at glory just to wander around the prairie all day long. Not that Stevie minded—riding was the ultimate fun— but she hoped Emily appreciated it, was all. She really hoped so.

"Switch places with me, Stevie," Lisa called. "That flat-footed horse of yours is kicking up enough dust to fill the Grand Canyon." She had no idea where on the ranch they were: For the past half hour she'd only been able to see the haze of brown dirt generated by Stewball's hooves. She was covered in dirt, and she was starting to itch.

"This flat-footed horse," Stevie said grandly, "is a showbiz superstar."

"Then maybe you ought to sign him up for ballet lessons to improve his movement. Unless, of course, you think he's kicking up dust on purpose, to bug me."

"I'm sure that's it." Stevie spoke to the horse: "Now, Stewball, sweetie, quit annoying your aunt Lisa." Stewball craned his neck around and looked at Lisa. He blinked at her apologetically and walked on. The dust stopped.

"Amazing," Lisa said.

"It's just that we've hit a spot of grass," Carole pointed out. "Stewball couldn't walk differently if he tried."

"Could too," Stevie said.

"Could not," Carole countered.

"I don't care, I'm just happy to be out of my dust cloud," Lisa said. "I was starting to feel like that comic-strip character Pig Pen."

"You look sort of like him," Emily observed. Lisa had dust streaked down her cheeks. It had settled into the folds of her clothing, and it lay across Chocolate's coat like a veil.

"Oh well, at least I'm on a horse," Lisa said cheerfully. If she'd been walking on foot behind Stewball, she probably would have been buried to her ears in dust. Lisa closed her eyes and for a moment dreamed of a steaming hot bubble bath and some nice fresh clothes—a skirt perhaps, her nice blue one, that went so well with that new ruffled shirt—*anything*, so long as it wasn't another pair of blue jeans.

She gasped and sat up, urging Chocolate forward. "What's wrong?" Carole asked. "Are you feeling okay?"

"I think my mother's spirit just invaded my body. It was horrifying."

"It's okay," Carole said soothingly. "You're out here at the ranch and on a horse."

Lisa thought that Chocolate's endless swaying motion was about to wear her hipbones out. "I know," she said. "I know exactly where I am."

Emily jogged over, grinning. "Isn't this fun?"

BEFORE DINNER LISA did manage a quick shower. With the dirt scrubbed out of her ears and the folds of her eyelids, she felt human again. When she came out of the bathroom, she saw Emily lying across her bunk with her eyes closed, a picture of exhaustion.

"Em, are you okay?" she asked. Since their first day, Emily seemed to have become used to spending long hours in the saddle and hadn't been overly tired. Still, today had been a riding marathon.

Emily opened one eye. "Do you think the Devines would care if I took my pillow into the ranch house and sat on it during dinner?" She

grinned wryly. "I think I'm beginning to understand the meaning of the term *saddle sore*."

Lisa nodded. "Me too."

Carole looked up from her bunk, where she
was trying to find one clean shirt to wear to dinner. "I saw these great cushiony fleece saddle
covers—"

"Don't tell us," Emily said. "Unless you saw
four of them in the Devines' tack room, I don't
want to hear a single word about them. I'll just
get envious."

Stevie had zipped into the bathroom when
Lisa had left it. Now she came out, scrubbing her
damp, clean hair with a towel. "Envious of what?
Us? For getting to ride all the time?"

Emily groaned and rolled over. "Oh, definitely," she said. Her sarcasm was unmistakable.
"I'm sure that's it."

Stevie made a sound through her nose. Given
that she and Stewball could be accepting Acad-
emy Awards right now for their wonderful, emo-
tionally compelling performances in the historic
Wild West Show, Emily ought to sound a little
more grateful.

Kate had gone to the ranch house to put on
some clean clothes, but she came back to walk

with the girls to dinner. "Good news," she said. "It's ham and beans and cornbread, and lots of it."

They hustled out the door. "That's the best news I've heard all day," Lisa said. "One thing about riding this much, it makes you hungry." She stumbled over a root. "Ouch!" she said, rubbing her hip.

"Are you okay?" Kate asked.

Lisa grinned. "Ever heard the phrase *saddle sore?*"

"*I* certainly know what it means," Stevie offered. She laughed, and suddenly all of them were laughing. The tension that had built up during their afternoon ride disappeared.

"I'd just like to point out," Emily said, grinning, "that I'm walking faster than all of you."

"I'd say that we were walking slowly to keep you company," Carole said, "except that it wouldn't be true. I can't move any faster."

"What happened to you being the worn-out one, anyway?" Stevie demanded.

Emily shook her head. "I don't know. I think maybe this trip has been good for me."

"You can say that again," Lisa replied. "It's been good for all of us."

"Ride, ride, ride," Stevie muttered. Lisa whacked Stevie's arm, and they all laughed.

They went into the ranch house and sat down. Emily stowed her crutches beneath her chair, as always. "Hey," she said, looking down at the place settings on the table, "are we expecting the honeymoon couples?"

"Count again," Mrs. Devine advised.

"Monica!" Kate said, with a delighted smile, just as Monica and her parents appeared in the door. "Hi, Monica! Come sit by me!"

Monica flushed, looking embarrassed and uncomfortable, but the soft smile she gave Kate was genuine. "Hi," she said. She fumbled with her crutches and the back of her chair, and for a moment, after she sat down, she seemed too upset to look at anyone. But, Carole thought, she had come to dinner, and that was a major improvement. Maybe they would be able to get her on a horse after all.

Mr. and Mrs. Hopkins fluttered around their daughter, looking anxious. "Let me take those for you, dear," her mother said, reaching for her crutches.

"Mom, I'm fine." Monica let the crutches drop to the floor. "Please sit down."

"Yes, please, dinner's ready," Mrs. Devine said in a friendly voice. They all sat and began to eat, but for a moment there was silence at the table. No one seemed to know just what to say. Carole felt she ought to break the ice, but how?

"I'm Carole Hanson," she said at last. "I'm one of Kate's friends from Virginia."

Monica looked shyly grateful. "I'm afraid I don't remember your names," she said. The rest of the girls introduced themselves in turn. Monica nodded and smiled, and then bent her head down, eating. She still seemed very uncomfortable, but it was clear to Carole that she was trying hard. *This must be so difficult for her*, Carole thought. She felt a wave of sympathy for Monica.

Across the table, Kate looked a bit uncomfortable, too. "We had the best ride today," she said at last. "We went everywhere—"

"—and she means *everywhere*," Stevie cut in.

"I've spent longer in the saddle in the last few days than I have out of it," Emily agreed. "Everyone else has been here before, Monica, but this is my first time. I've never seen anything like this countryside."

Monica looked interested, but Mr. Hopkins cleared his throat awkwardly. "Can we please not talk about riding?" he asked. He cleared his throat again and made a small motion toward his daughter. "Please."

Monica flushed and looked at her plate again. Carole wondered if Monica really minded if they talked about riding. After all, she thought, recalling their week, what else was there to talk about?

The phone rang. Mr. Devine went to answer it, while the others at the table sat in silence once again. Carole tried to think of something besides horses to talk about, but the more she tried, the more she could think only about horses. Kate looked upset. Monica looked as though she, too, was trying to think of a topic for conversation.

"Oh, well, Harry, that's nice of you." Mr. Devine's voice carried clearly into the dining room. "I know our ordinary guests would love it, but you've never seen anything like these friends of Kate's. All these girls want to do is ride. We haven't been able to get them out of the saddle all week. Thanks anyway. Bye." He hung up and came back to the table, smiling cheerfully. "Sorry for the interruption," he said.

"Who was that?" Mrs. Devine asked.

Mr. Devine buttered a piece of cornbread before he spoke. "Harry Foreman, from up the road. He organizes white-water rafting trips on the river, girls, and since I'd told him you were here he wanted to invite you out tomorrow. He's got a raft that's nearly empty. But I knew you'd rather ride. Right?" He looked around at their solemn faces and put the piece of cornbread down. "Right?"

"Right," Carole said slowly. She tried not to remember that she'd always wanted to go white-water rafting.

"Right," Lisa said dutifully, trying to sound like she meant it. White-water rafting wasn't something her parents would ever try. If she didn't go now, when would she get another chance?

"Right," Stevie said, even more reluctantly than Lisa. She had to go along with The Saddle Club, of course, but, oh, rafting sounded exciting!

Emily chewed her food and swallowed. She set her fork gently on the edge of her plate. She seemed to be thinking hard. Finally she said, "I'm sorry. I know you guys would rather ride, but I wouldn't. I think white-water rafting sounds like a blast."

To everyone's surprise, Monica leaned across the table eagerly. "It is a blast," she said. "I've done it before, and it's the *biggest* blast in the world. Let's go!"

"ACTUALLY," STEVIE SAID, with a giant exhalation of breath, "I'd *love* to go white-water rafting!"

"Me too!" Carole said.

"Me three—er, six!" Lisa said, counting quickly. She started to laugh. Emily and Monica were grinning at each other across the table. Stevie and Kate were cheering.

"I'll call Harry back," Mr. Devine said. "I see I've made a mistake." He was smiling.

"A big mistake, Dad," Kate said. "Tomorrow we'll trade our saddles for paddles!"

"I'll show you all what to do," Monica offered. "It's not difficult."

"Monica." Mrs. Hopkins voice was low but urgent. "Monica, honey, you can't go."

"Of course I can," Monica said.

"If Mr. Foreman had room for five people, I'm sure he can find room for six," Kate said.

"Darling, it would just be too dangerous," Mr. Hopkins said, agreeing with his wife.

Monica tossed her hair over her shoulder. Her eyes were blazing. "Dangerous for whom?" she said. Lisa blinked. It seemed to her that Monica was coming alive before her very eyes.

Both Mr. and Mrs. Hopkins seemed flustered. Lisa could tell they were only trying to protect their daughter.

"I'll be sitting in a boat!" Monica practically shouted. "I'll be wearing a life vest! How many legs do I need?"

Stevie started to say something, but Lisa jabbed her into silence. This was between Monica and her parents.

"It'll be a big change for you," Monica's mother said. "It's not that we don't want you to do things—we just don't want you to get hurt. Your balance will be different now." She paused. "It's not going to be the same."

"It's *never* going to be the same," Monica said,

in a quieter tone. "I won't get hurt, at least I'll try not to. But I really want to do this. I've got to start doing things. I am different now. I'm going to be different forever." She bit her lip. "Please, Mom."

Mrs. Hopkins brushed a tear from her eye. "Okay," she said at last. "We've always trusted your judgment. We've always been able to. If you want to do this, go ahead." Mr. Hopkins nodded.

"Thank you," Monica whispered.

Mr. Devine came back into the room, beaming. "All set," he said. "There's even room for Christine, if she wants to come."

"All right!" Monica said. Lisa didn't realize until that moment that Monica must know Christine from earlier trips to the ranch.

"I'll call her," Kate said.

"Why don't we ride over and ask her instead?" Stevie asked. Lisa caught her breath. For a moment she thought Stevie had forgotten about Monica, but then, looking at her friend, Lisa realized that Stevie knew exactly what she was asking.

"You too, Monica," Stevie said. "It's an easy ride. Come with us."

Monica flushed again. "I know, I've ridden to

Christine's house," she said. She began to stammer. "I—I'd like to—but no—I don't—"

Emily half stood, then fell to the ground. Her crutches became tangled in the legs of her chair, and the chair fell on top of her with a humongous clatter. "Blast," she said from beneath the rubble. "All I was trying to do was stand up. Maybe I'm not Superwoman after all. Lisa, could you move the stupid chair?"

Lisa picked the chair up and gave Emily a hand. "Thanks," Emily said. She set her arms firmly in the cuffs of her crutches. "That's better."

"Monica," Stevie said, pressing for an answer. Lisa looked up and saw to her surprise that Monica and her parents were staring at Emily. Emily stared back.

"What's wrong with you?" Monica asked her.

"I fell over," Emily said indignantly. "I lost my balance and crashed. Please tell me it's never happened to you."

Monica's face softened in apology. "No," she said. "I'm sorry, that's not what I meant. Why do you have crutches? Why are you wearing those leg braces?"

"I have cerebral palsy," Emily said. From her tone Lisa knew that Emily was still miffed.

Monica looked amazed and her parents had their mouths open like fish. "But you can't have cerebral palsy," Mrs. Hopkins said. "You're the little girl we saw galloping all over the prairie."

Emily's anger turned to astonishment, and then to something like happiness. She laughed out loud. "You really didn't notice!" she said. "You never *realized* I look different!"

"But you *don't*," Monica said. "I mean, I guess you do now, a little bit, if I look close."

"Give me a break," Emily said. "As if you can't see these crutches a mile away."

"But I didn't see them when you were sitting down. I guess when you were outside my cabin, I just wasn't paying attention. And you ride as well as your friends."

"See," Stevie cut in. "Emily's had C.P. her whole life, and she rides great. You already know how to ride, Monica. You can still do it."

Monica paused. She seemed to be thinking hard. Her parents, Lisa saw, looked as though learning about Emily's disability had shocked them into silence. Now maybe they wouldn't be so overprotective of Monica.

Monica pushed her hair back behind her ears. She gathered her crutches and slowly stood. "I don't know if I can still ride," she said, looking at Emily but speaking to them all, "but I think it's time to find out."

THEY LEFT THEIR dinners on their plates. At Monica's request, Mr. and Mrs. Hopkins stayed behind, too. Only the six girls headed out to the barn.

"Which horse can I ride?" Monica asked, as they went through the doors.

"Which horse do you want to ride?" Kate asked her.

Monica shrugged. "Oh . . . any horse will be fine." She looked around in surprise. "I don't remember you guys keeping so many horses inside."

"These are the ones we've been riding," Stevie explained. "We left them inside to eat their grain; we'll turn them out with the herd later. Have you met Stewball?" She patted the piebald's face. "Stewball, meet your aunt Monica."

Monica laughed. "I've met him. That horse is too weird for me."

"John!" Kate shouted.

"Up here!" John shouted from the hayloft.

121

"Can you get a horse out for Monica?"

"Sure!" John came down the ladder. He grabbed a halter and went out to the paddock where the other riding horses were. In a moment he was back, leading a pretty buckskin mare.

"Buttercup!" Monica said. She hurried forward and leaned against the mare. "Oh, Buttercup! Can I really ride her, Kate?"

"She's been waiting for you," Kate said. "You always ride Buttercup."

"That's right, I do," Monica said. "Beautiful Buttercup. Okay, where's my saddle?"

"You'll need this." Emily handed Monica a riding crop. "It's mine, but I've got an extra one. Use it in place of your leg."

"She'll understand you," John added. "Kate and I have been working with her."

Monica's eyes sparkled with tears, but the rest of her expression was grimly determined. Waving off John's help, she saddled up Buttercup while the others readied their own horses. Then John held Buttercup while Monica made her way up the mounting ramp. She removed her crutches and set them down, then hopped a few steps to Buttercup's side. Leaning her weight against the saddle, she slid her left foot into the stirrup, then swung her right knee over the saddle. "Okay," she said to John, as she gathered up the reins. She clucked to Buttercup, who took a few steps forward.

"Okay?" Kate asked.

"Okay?" Monica's laugh rang out across the ranch. "Better than okay! This feels like heaven!"

11

"I sure hope," Stevie said, delicately extracting herself from the very back of the ranch station wagon, "that the rafts have more room than this car." She gave Lisa a hand. The raft launch site was larger and busier than she'd imagined. There were at least a dozen large inflatable rafts, and tons of people were putting on helmets and life preservers. There was even a small supply store.

"I don't know if I agree," Christine replied. "If we're packed in tightly, it won't be as easy for us to fall out. Thanks for the ride, Colonel Devine."

Colonel Devine nodded. "You're welcome. I'll

go find Harry and tell him that you're here." He walked toward the store.

"Thanks," Stevie and Carole called after him.

"Thanks," Emily echoed, swinging out of the back door. To Christine she added, "I don't think we need to worry about falling out. White-water rapids are graded from class one to class six, and these don't get higher than class three."

Christine laughed. "You sound like an expert."

"I've been talking to one the whole way here. Right, Monica?" Emily leaned over to look back into the car. "Monica? Are you okay?"

The tall girl was sitting still in the center of the seat. Her face was pale and uneasy. "What's wrong?" Emily asked. The whole way there— ever since her ride the night before, in fact— Monica had been happy and energetic. Now suddenly she looked frozen again.

"What's wrong?" Carole asked, coming to stand next to Emily. The others gathered around.

"I just didn't expect there to be so many people—so many strangers." Monica took a deep breath. "Oh well," she said. She picked up her crutches and eased herself out of the car, glancing around nervously as she did so. A few people in some of the other groups looked over toward them. Some of them looked twice when they noticed Monica was missing a leg.

Monica saw them looking. She shook her head. "I don't know if I can do this," she whispered. "Maybe I should go back home with Mr. Devine."

"Monica!" Stevie cajoled. "We need you! You're the only one who's done this before."

"We'll have a great time once we get started," Kate added. "Just like you did riding yesterday. Getting started is the worst part."

"I don't know," Monica said again. She sat down on the edge of the car seat.

The Saddle Club exchanged grim glances. They couldn't *make* Monica come. "Please come," Lisa said softly.

Emily leaned against the side of the car. "Monica," she said, looking her straight in the eye, "people are going to be staring at you for the rest of your life. It will be easier once you get your prosthetic leg, because you won't look so different then, but some people will still stare, and there's nothing you can do about it." She took a deep breath. "People stare at me all the time," she continued. "Some of the people you

126

think are staring at you right now are probably staring at me."

"They're probably staring at both of us," Monica said.

Emily shrugged. "Probably."

Lisa realized once again the pain this sort of thing caused Emily. When Emily had first come riding at Pine Hollow, a certain insensitive rider named Veronica diAngelo had made some very rude remarks. Emily had been so upset she cried. By now Lisa had spent so much time around Emily that she never paid attention to strangers staring, no more than she paid attention to Emily's spastic muscles. Emily, Lisa thought, never stopped noticing.

"Okay," Monica said, her eyes fixed on Emily, "what do I do? How do you deal with other people's reactions? How do you keep it from bothering you?"

"I don't," Emily said.

Monica blinked. Clearly, Lisa thought, that wasn't the answer she was expecting.

"It always bothers me when people stare," Emily said. "I hate it. It's even worse when people act like I'm stupid because I can't walk well. But I learned a long time ago that I can't help what other people do. I can only help what I do. And I want to ride, and I want to go white-water rafting."

Monica nodded. Some of the strain left her face. "That makes sense," she said. "It's just not easy."

"Nope," Emily said.

"At least, today, you're surrounded by friends," Kate said.

Monica smiled. "I know that." She took a deep breath and stood back up. "I'll go," she said.

"Good!" Kate gave Monica a hug. "I'm so glad!"

Lisa took half a step forward to hug Monica, too, but a tug on her shirt sleeve pulled her back. "Saddle Club meeting," Stevie hissed in her ear. "Carole, you too."

"Now?" Lisa whispered back, as Stevie hurried them both into the little supply store.

"Now," Stevie said. "But I don't need you as much as I need your money. How much do you have?"

"About five dollars, but why—"

"Hand it over," Stevie said. Lisa did. Carole took a few crumpled bills out of her pocket, too, and Stevie marched to the cash register.

128

Carole and Lisa exchanged puzzled looks. "I guess I just won't ask," Lisa said.

"Guess not," Carole said.

In a moment Stevie was back with a small paper bag under her arm. "Now," she said, tipping the contents of the bag into her hands, "you two hold still."

Two minutes later The Saddle Club returned to the station wagon, where Mr. Devine was helping Kate, Christine, Monica, and Emily adjust their life vests. "Stevie!" Kate shrieked when she saw them. "Lisa! Carole! What happened to you?" All three girls were painted in outrageous stripes of neon orange, green, and blue. Stevie had a blue sun painted on each cheek. Carole had neon green whiskers. Lisa was polka-dotted. All three of them had tiger stripes running up their arms as well.

"Hold still," Stevie commanded. She took one of the three tubes of colored zinc sunblock she'd bought and gave Kate a long orange squiggle down her nose. Lisa added green triangles, and Carole striped her arms blue.

"Now Monica," Stevie continued. Soon Monica, Christine, and Emily were equally well decorated.

129

"It's festive," Christine said, looking at the stripes encircling her wrists. "Does it have a purpose?"

Stevie grinned. "If anyone's going to stare at any one of us," she said, "they're going to stare at all of us."

"Hold still, Stevie," Monica said. "I think I want to add another stripe to your nose."

"WOW," CAROLE SAID in dismay. "When they say sunblock, they mean sun*block*."

"I know," Lisa said ruefully. "I actually thought I had a pretty good tan before today. I'm surprised we got as much sun as we did."

"The reflections off the water intensify the rays," Monica explained.

"I'd say so," Stevie said glumly. When they had washed the neon sunblock off, they found that the skin beneath it was now a shade lighter than the non-sunblocked skin. In other words, Kate still had a squiggle down her nose. Monica had stars on her cheeks, and Stevie had sun shapes. Carole had whiskers. Lisa had dots. All of them had striped arms.

"Oh well," Stevie said cheerfully. "It'll probably fade before we get back to Pine Hollow."

They were all sitting in The Saddle Club's bunkhouse. At least, Carole and Monica were sitting. Lisa, Emily, and Stevie were lying down. Rafting, they discovered, was even more exercise than riding. It was also nearly as much fun.

"Swoosh!" Stevie said in an undertone, and the others laughed. Whenever a wave had flooded the raft—which had been roughly every thirty seconds—they'd all yelled "Swoosh!"

"Wasn't that great?" Monica asked.

"Yep," Stevie replied. "How're your bruises, Lisa?" Of all of them, Lisa had been the only one to fall out of the raft.

"Not bad," Lisa said. "How're yours?"

"They only hurt when I touch them." Stevie hadn't actually fallen in—but when Lisa had gone overboard, Stevie had dived in to save her.

"I don't think I'd be bruised if you hadn't jumped on me," Lisa continued.

"I couldn't let you drown," Stevie protested.

"I wasn't going to drown! The water was only three feet deep!"

Kate banged on the door. Carole jumped up to open it, and Kate and Christine came in with their arms full of food and sleeping bags.

"Are you sure there's room for me in here?"

Monica asked, looking doubtfully at the crowded bunkhouse. "I could stay with my parents."

"We're sure," Kate replied. "Give us a break, will you? We wanted you with us all week."

"It's a slumber party!" Christine yelled. She opened one of the grocery bags she'd carried in. "I've got the popcorn popper! Kate, where's the popcorn?"

"Somewhere," Kate answered, looking through the other bags.

"We can use Lisa's hair dryer to melt the butter," Stevie offered.

"Does she always have ideas like this?" Monica asked Emily.

"Always," Emily said. "Stevie, I'm going to call you Sunshine."

Stevie blushed slightly, and the pale sun shapes on her cheeks turned pink. "If I'm Sunshine, you're Blockhead," she retorted. "You've got squares on your forehead."

"Squiggle," Monica said to Kate.

"Freckles," Kate said to Lisa.

Lisa looked at Carole's whiskers. "Here, kitty, kitty!" she called. Carole threw a sock at Lisa.

"Oh no!" Lisa cried in horror. "It's one of Stevie's socks!" She threw a pillow at Stevie.

"Pillow fight!" Emily cried, whacking Christine.

When they finished their fight, and Kate was declared Queen Pillow Thrower and Squiggle Nose, they rearranged the room so that sleeping bags for Monica and Christine would fit on the floor. Christine popped corn while Stevie melted butter in the glass from the bathroom. Emily opened sodas and passed them around.

Lisa flexed her foot and pointed it. She had a bruise on her shin, but it didn't hurt very much. She felt tired from the day's exertions, but also, in some strange way, refreshed. "You know," she commented, "once in a while I think it's actually good to get a little break from riding. Rafting was a lot of fun."

"I guess I am glad we decided to go," Carole agreed, "even if it did mean we couldn't ride for a day."

"Okay," Christine said. "Explain something to me, please. Every other time you guys have come here, you've spent at least a day doing something else. The time you helped with my mom's Halloween party you hardly rode at all. Why were you so obsessed with riding this trip?"

Kate looked amused. Emily looked dumbfounded. "Aren't they always this obsessed?" she asked.

The Saddle Club looked a little uncomfortable.

"No," Christine said. "They always ride a lot—we all do—but geez, this week was ridiculous! I would have come with you guys yesterday, but I was tired out from the day before."

"I thought you never did anything but ride," Emily said to Stevie.

Stevie started laughing. "We mostly ride," she said. "I promise, Em. But this time—we thought you were only interested in riding."

"You did?" Emily started laughing. "But I thought *you* were only interested in riding!"

"You mean I didn't really have to be on that horse for eighteen hours in a row?" Lisa asked.

"Stewball and I could have made history," Stevie said with a groan.

"We could have gone to the horse auction!" Carole added.

"Don't blame me for this," Emily said. "Whenever you guys talked about the Bar None, you talked about riding, riding, riding. You never talked about doing anything else."

"Well, of course not," Carole said. "Riding is the most important thing."

"If you wanted to do something else, Em, why didn't you say so?" Stevie asked. "We would have listened."

"I could ask you the same question," Emily retorted.

"You seemed so excited about spending the whole week on a horse," Stevie explained. "You've never gotten to do that before—and we've been out here a bunch. Plus, we really do ride almost all the time."

Emily nodded. "I didn't want to mess up the stuff you guys usually do," she said. "We have to do some things differently because of my C.P.— like choose the right picnic spots—so I didn't want to ask you to do other things differently, too."

"Oh well," Lisa said. "Really, what would we have done differently? We couldn't have gone to the dog show and the horse auction and the Wild West Show and white-water rafting—then we really wouldn't have had enough time to ride."

"Rafting was the best," Carole said. "We're lucky it came last."

135

The others agreed. "Man," Emily said, "by last night my seat was really starting to ache!"

Carole laughed. "Fleece saddle covers," she said. "Tell Colonel Devine about them, Emily; he's listening to whatever you suggest. Tell him he'll need one for every saddle before our next visit."

Stevie yawned and stretched. She took another handful of popcorn. "Rafting was a good cure for saddle soreness," she said. "I'm ready to ride again."

"I'm more than ready," Monica said. She climbed into her sleeping bag. "Do you have the alarm set right, Kate? We don't want to be late."

"That's right!" Carole said. "I almost forgot!"

"Don't worry," Kate assured them. "I know what time the sun rises." She put the alarm clock on her cot next to her pillow. They hastily got into bed. Stevie turned out the light.

In the darkness Emily yawned. "I can't wait for morning!" she said. The others agreed.

12

IN THE EARLY morning darkness, seven girls on horseback climbed toward the sun. The horses' breathing made rhythmic rushing noises. The wind was still. The only other sounds were the occasional clink of a horseshoe against a stone.

Carole felt Berry's warm, broad back smooth beneath her. She sat tall and proud. She loved riding bareback. She loved riding. She was entirely happy.

Above her, a scattering of stars still shone in the indigo sky. In front of her, behind the hill they were now climbing, she knew the sky was beginning to lighten. But they had time yet before dawn.

"Oh," Monica said softly. Carole turned her head. Even in the dim light, she could see that Monica wasn't in any sort of trouble. Riding bareback was harder than riding with a saddle, but Monica had done it before. The horses were walking slowly. The girls had been riding nearly an hour.

"How do you feel, Emily?" Lisa asked, moving Chocolate a little closer to Spot's side.

Emily grinned. "I feel great. This is fantastic." Emily had never ridden bareback before. She had also, she told them that morning, never ridden in the dark before, but Kate assured her that the horses would be surefooted. Emily hadn't seemed worried.

"You look great," Lisa told her. "I remember my first bareback sunrise ride. I really hadn't been riding very long, and going bareback made me nervous at first. But I caught on."

"It's slippery," Emily said. "I've had to grab mane about six times. And I never realized horses were so warm. I think it's loosening my leg muscles."

"Another form of therapy," Lisa joked.

Emily chuckled. "Wait until I try it with P.C."

"We're almost there," Kate said. "We're in plenty of time." A few final steps brought them to the crest of the hill. They halted their horses on the summit; in front of them, the valley swept down into a wide expanse before rising again into distant mountains. The bottom of the sky had turned rosy pink, but the mountains and valley were still shrouded in darkness.

The horses waited peacefully. The girls waited expectantly. "Here it comes," Kate said. The first bright ray of sunshine shot over the top of the distant range.

"Wow!" Emily said. "I always thought sunrise was a more gradual thing."

"Maybe in Virginia," Kate said. "Not here." Soon the eastern sky was flooded with rose and yellow light. The face of their hill began to glow with light, and, gradually, as the sun rose, light drifted down the valley.

"Every time I see this, it's more beautiful than the last," Carole said.

"I told you it was worth getting up at four A.M. for," Stevie said to Emily.

"You were right," Emily replied. "But I always thought it sounded worthwhile." Birds woke up, and soon the air was full of sounds. The wind began to blow.

Finally Kate turned Moonglow. "Time for breakfast," she said. They started back.

When they were nearly home, Emily challenged them. "A race," she said. "Let's have a race. Monica?"

Monica looked disconcerted. Carole was sure that Monica's balance wasn't up to bareback galloping, not yet, and she was equally sure that Emily's wasn't, either. She opened her mouth to say so when Emily grinned and said, "A walking race. First horse home wins, but anyone who trots is out."

Monica grinned. "That sounds like a good bareback race." She tapped her crop gently behind her leg to perk up Buttercup's walk. Buttercup responded with a slight increase in speed.

Lisa tried to motivate Chocolate, but the mare seemed to have fallen asleep. Lisa clucked and squeezed with her legs. Chocolate didn't seem to notice. "This is a bad time for a nap," Lisa told her. "Stevie," she continued, "what are you doing?" Stevie had gathered the reins short. She wrapped her legs around Stewball's barrel.

"Dressage," Stevie said grandly. "Behold an

extended walk." She signaled to Stewball. He promptly jogged.

"Thank you," Lisa told her. "Now I can't be last even if Chocolate lies down for a nap."

Stevie good-naturedly rode over to Lisa. "Her eyes are closing," she reported. "Chocolate! Wake up! Think about oats! Think about hay!"

"Arahyh!" Christine muttered in disgust, behind them.

"What happened?" Lisa asked.

"He jogged," Christine said. "Just one stride!"

"Oh well," Stevie said. "Come up and join the losers brigade."

"Speak for yourself," Lisa retorted. "If everyone else jogs, Chocolate and I will win."

Christine eyed Chocolate. "She's not going to jog, that's for sure."

In the end, Kate won by a large margin. "But Moonglow's my horse," she said. "I know her really well, and she listens to me."

"What's my excuse?" Christine asked, laughing.

"It's like you, Kate, to credit Moonglow," Emily added. "As if your superior horsemanship didn't have anything to do with it." The Saddle Club had told Emily all about Kate's illustrious show background. Emily could see for herself what a good rider Kate was.

"Well," Monica said, with a big grin, "I'm not going to give Buttercup any credit for my second-place finish. It was *all* due to my superior horsemanship."

"Oh, of course," Emily said, rolling her eyes. Monica laughed. She dismounted and hugged Buttercup for a long time.

"Riding feels so good," she said.

"At this point," Stevie said, "breakfast might feel even better."

When they trooped into the dining room, Monica's parents looked both startled and proud to see their daughter up so early. "Getting ready to ride?" Mrs. Hopkins asked.

"Mom, look at my jeans," Monica said. "That's horsehair they're covered with. We've been riding for two hours already."

"Bareback," Emily added proudly.

"We're famished," Stevie said, as they all sat down.

Once they'd consumed half a dozen pancakes each, they were capable of speech again. "Okay,"

Kate said, still chewing, "let's make plans. You guys will need to leave the ranch at three o'clock this afternoon. How long will it take you to pack up?"

Stevie speared another pancake off the platter. "Twenty minutes, tops."

"Okay." Kate checked her watch. "It'll take half an hour to take care of the horses at the end of the day, so we can ride until ten after two. It's six forty-five now—"

"Lunch," Stevie pleaded.

"Picnic," Emily said crisply.

"Good idea! We can make that while we let the horses digest their breakfasts."

"If we hurry making the picnic," Lisa suggested, "we'll have time to pack this morning. Then we can ride until two-thirty."

Carole grinned. "That's using your head, Lisa. Where haven't we been yet? We need to show Emily the island—"

"What about Pulpit Rock?" Monica cut in. "I want to see that."

"They've already been there," Kate explained. "Monica, you and I have all day tomorrow to go everywhere they've already been."

"If you can go everywhere we've been in only one day, we'll award you the golden fleece saddle cover," Carole said.

"We won't try," Christine said. "But Kate, I'll come if you'll let me."

"Of course," Monica said. "Today, too, I hope."

"Of course," Christine said.

Mrs. Hopkins cut in with a happy smile on her face. "Perhaps your father and I will come tomorrow, too," she said.

Monica considered it. "I don't mind," she said at last, "but we're going to be spending all day in the saddle. You might get a little sore."

Colonel Devine teased them. "I thought two days ago that you all were looking a little sore. I thought maybe you were getting tired of riding. Now look at you! I'm going to have to pry you out of your saddles with a crowbar and carry you screaming onto the plane. What happened?"

Carole looked at him with wide eyes. "Colonel Devine," she said, "we didn't ride for almost thirty-two hours!"

"Good-bye!" Emily hugged Kate and Mrs. Devine. "Thank you so much for having me out here. I had the best time of my whole life."

Kate's mom gave Emily another hug. "Thank you for all the help you gave us. Come back soon."

"Oh, I hope I can!" Emily followed The Saddle Club up the ramp of the tiny plane. Colonel Devine shut and fastened the door, and Emily sat down with her friends. "I can't believe it's been six days already," she said. "Time went by so quickly."

"Vacation time works differently than ordinary time," Stevie explained.

"Oh, I know," Emily said. "Just like riding time goes by much faster than cleaning-tack time."

"Which is faster than do-your-homework time or wash-the-dishes time."

"Homework!" Carole exclaimed. "Don't talk about school. That's months away." She pressed her face against the window as the plane took off. Soon Kate, her mother, and the tiny airstrip had all faded into the clouds.

"I'll be a little bit glad to be home, I guess," Emily admitted. "I miss P.C. After all this riding, I think I'm a lot stronger now. I wonder if P.C. will be able to notice the difference."

"I bet Ms. Payne will notice," Lisa said. Ms. Payne was Emily's riding instructor.

"Oh, I know she will," Emily said. "I think she'll be thrilled for me, especially after I tell her about our bareback ride and everything."

"Think she'll notice your face?" Lisa asked with a sly grin. The effects of the sunscreen hadn't yet faded. They were returning to Pine Hollow striped, squiggled, and spotted.

"I'm a little embarrassed," Carole cut in. "Dots

and shapes are one thing, but I've got *cat whiskers*."

"I'm going to tell everyone it was a secret Native American ritual I went through," Emily said with a grin. "I'll see how many people I can get to believe me."

"Zero," said Stevie.

"At least six," countered Emily.

Stevie held out her hand. "I bet you can't. Loser has to ride without stirrups for three days."

Emily shook. "It's a bet." She leaned back in her seat. "I'm certainly going to tell everyone at Free Rein about the Bar None. Maybe some people will want to go on vacation there. The Devines were really making it nice for disabled people."

"You helped them," Stevie pointed out.

"I don't think I helped them a whole free vacation's worth," Emily said. "I definitely got the good end of the deal." She unzipped a pocket on her backpack. "Anybody want some licorice? Oh, yuck!" She pulled out a dark, wizened object.

"That's licorice?" Stevie asked. "No thank you."

"No," Emily said sadly. "This is a carrot. I

147

brought it to give to Spot—to whatever horse I was going to be riding."

Lisa started laughing. "You brought a carrot from home?"

"I meant to give it to him right away on the first day," Emily explained. "I just forgot. Look—it didn't mold at all, it just dried up. It's kind of interesting."

"Prehistoric," said Carole. "Like Mrs. Devine's biscuits."

"And probably about as edible." Emily wrapped the carrot in a tissue and returned it to her pack. She pulled out several sticks of licorice. "These were in a plastic bag. They didn't touch the carrot—I promise." The girls accepted the licorice hesitantly.

"Geez," Emily said. "Just eat it. It won't kill you."

They sat and munched in silence for a few moments. "Tastes all right," Lisa said. She crossed her legs and grimaced slightly. "That bruise." She rolled up her jeans to look at it. "It looks like it's getting bigger."

"Rafting was worth it," said Carole.

"Of course." Lisa looked thoughtful. "You know, Emily, you did help the Devines, but I

148

think the person you helped most was Monica. We all tried to get her back in the saddle, but you're the one who did it."

"By falling down," Emily reminded her. "It wasn't exactly brilliant. And I didn't do it on purpose, either."

"*Not* by falling down," Carole said firmly. She leaned forward. "You helped by galloping across the prairie—by showing the Hopkinses what you could do. And you're the one who convinced Monica to go white-water rafting. If you hadn't known what to say, she probably would have gone home."

Emily looked a little embarrassed. "I only knew what to say because I knew she must be feeling the way I feel sometimes," she said. "Monica would have figured everything out without me. It just might have taken her a little more time. And her adjustment isn't over. Lots of things are still going to be hard for her."

"But not the Bar None," Lisa said. "She got that back, and Kate's friendship, too. I would have felt really bad for Kate if Monica had stayed in her bunkhouse the whole week. Kate was so upset."

"That's another thing," Emily said. "If I

149

helped her at all, it was only because she did come out of her bunkhouse. Remember? She came to dinner. She decided to join us first."

"Anyway," Stevie said, "it worked out great. There's just one other thing that's been bugging me. Em, promise us that next time, if you want to do some of the other things besides ride, you'll tell us."

Emily looked around at them with a serious expression on her face. "Of course," she said. "I can always tell you if I don't want to do something. Only"—she turned a little pink—"I consider you guys such good friends that I didn't want to disappoint you. The most important thing to me was that you guys have a great time."

Stevie smiled. "That's the way we felt, too— that's why we didn't say anything to you. We wanted you to have a great time."

Emily grinned. "That's not bad," she said.

"No." Stevie winked at Carole, who started rummaging through her own backpack.

"Here it is." Carole pulled out a small box and handed it to Emily. Emily opened it.

"It's beautiful!" Inside was a tiny silver pin of a horse in full gallop.

"When we started The Saddle Club, we

bought matching pins," Lisa explained. "This one is a little different, but it's Native American art, so we thought it would remind you of our trip West. Christine picked it out for us.

"The Saddle Club has two rules," Lisa continued. "Members have to be horse-crazy, and they have to be willing to help each other out." She paused. "That's us, and that's you."

Emily looked up with her eyes aglow. "You want me to be part of The Saddle Club?" she asked.

Stevie gave her a hug. "You already are," she said. "You have been for at least the last week. All we're doing is making it official."

Emily pinned the galloping horse to her sweatshirt. "I accept," she said.

ABOUT THE AUTHOR

BONNIE BRYANT is the author of many books for young readers, including novelizations of movie hits such as *Teenage Mutant Ninja Turtles* and *Honey, I Blew Up the Kid,* written under her married name, B. B. Hiller.

Ms. Bryant began writing The Saddle Club in 1986. Although she had done some riding before that, she intensified her studies then and found herself learning right along with her characters Stevie, Carole, and Lisa. She claims that they are all much better riders than she is.

Ms. Bryant was born and raised in New York City. She still lives there, in Greenwich Village, with her two sons.